## MAGEPUNK

*Art of the Genre* represents a huge shared world called *The Nameless Realms*, a place that spans thirteen extraordinary Ages of Man. Each category of fiction in this fantastic world has its own specialized medallion that is 'active' in the upper right corner of each book, thus allowing you to easily tell what specific genre you're purchasing. In the case of The Gun Kingdoms, you're about to enter an age of Magepunk, set in the Eleventh Age of Man, so the medallion you see above is the symbol for all books in that field.

# GUN KINGDOMS

### SCOTT TAYLOR

*Illustrated by*
### DAVID DEITRICK

**Gun Kingdoms**
Copyright © 2012 Art of the Genre

Printed and bound in the United States of America 9 8 7 6 5 4 3 2 1

First edition: May 2012

ISBN: 978-0-9853328-4-6

This is a work of fiction. All characters, places and events portrayed in this publication are either fictitious or used fictitiously.

Cover and Interior Illustrations: David Deitrick
Copy Editor Extreme: Joshua Villines
Graphic Design: Jeff Laubenstein
Book Design: John Woolley
Writing Instructor: Terri-Lynne DeFino
Sounding Board: John O'Neill

Art of the Genre
217 Palos Verdes Blvd,
#217 Redondo Beach,
CA 90277

artofthegenre.myshopify.com

Ordering Information:
For details, contact the publisher at the address above.

*I want to dedicate this book to my mother, Sandra Taylor. For a single mother, she was a full family to her only child, and everything I am today was because of all that she gave up to see me succeed as a man.*

*I'd also like to put in one last thank you to all the fans on Kickstarter who made this dream a reality with their generous donations and to artist David Deitrick who placed a ship in my mind that I couldn't help but write a novel about.*

# CONTENTS

CONTENTS ....................................................... vii

ACKNOWLEDGEMENTS ..................................... xi

CHAPTER ONE ................................................. 1

CHAPTER TWO ................................................ 7

CHAPTER THREE ............................................. 15

CHAPTER FOUR............................................... 23

CHAPTER FIVE ................................................ 31

CHAPTER SIX................................................... 37

CHAPTER SEVEN ............................................. 45

CHAPTER EIGHT ............................................. 53

CHAPTER NINE ............................................... 61

CHAPTER TEN.................................................. 69

CHAPTER ELEVEN ........................................... 77

CHAPTER TWELVE .......................................... 85

CHAPTER THIRTEEN ....................................... 93

CHAPTER FOURTEEN....................................... 101

CHAPTER FIFTEEN .......................................... 109

CHAPTER SIXTEEN .......................................... 117

CHAPTER SEVENTEEN...................................... 127

CHAPTER EIGHTEEN ....................................... 135

CHAPTER NINETEEN ....................................... 143

CHAPTER TWENTY........................................... 149

CHAPTER TWENTY-ONE................................... 157

CHAPTER TWENTY-TWO .................................. 165

# FOREWORD

First, concerning the style of The Gun Kingdoms... As with all my Kickstarter inspired fiction, I wrote this book to tell a particular type of tale. To achieve this I wanted to place something into the story telling process that allowed fans a chance to hear directly from the main characters involved. At the beginning of each chapter there is a little aside from the character that controls the point of view for the chapter, and it's addressed directly to you, the reader. Certainly, the character has no idea who or what you are, just that they are being observed for whatever reason, so at some points they might be trying to figure out what you are, or place a title to you, and in other's they're simply talking because they know someone is listening.

To me, I always was intrigued by what motivated characters in books or what they might be thinking, so I hope you enjoy this aspect of the book, and if not, just skip to the meat of the chapter beneath each opening header.

Secondly, this book was created through the Kickstarter funding platform, so it wouldn't exist without the fans that supported it. I promised them steampunk, or in this case magepunk, and I hope I've delivered that. Inside the pages there are so many things I've enjoyed as a fan of various genres, and it's my hope those reading will be able to place some of the hidden tributes and feel I was going for.

This book was a labor of love by both myself and artist David R. Deitrick, who has worked his entire career building fantastic worlds, and Gun Kingdoms is no different. It's our profound pleasure to be able to bring this book to you, and we hope beyond all reckoning that you enjoy reading it as much as we did creating it.

# ACKNOWLEDGEMENTS

With heartfelt thanks to all our Kickstarter backers!

Michael Zabkar, Sean Veira, Don Schlaich, Adam Thoume, Lance Runkle, Tim Caswell

Eric Anderson, Gene, Francis Morehouse

Nick M, Chris Thompson, Kyle Pinches, Sharon 'Ladywolf' Irwin , Jeffrey Barnes, Peter M. Poulsen, Jeroen Bessems

Rhel, Mark 'Everdark' Timm, Mikael Olofsson

Mark Mastromarino, Andrew Findlay

Jason 'Doc' White, Noah, Paul Jarman

And a special shout out to Alyssa Faden, our Platinum Sponsor!

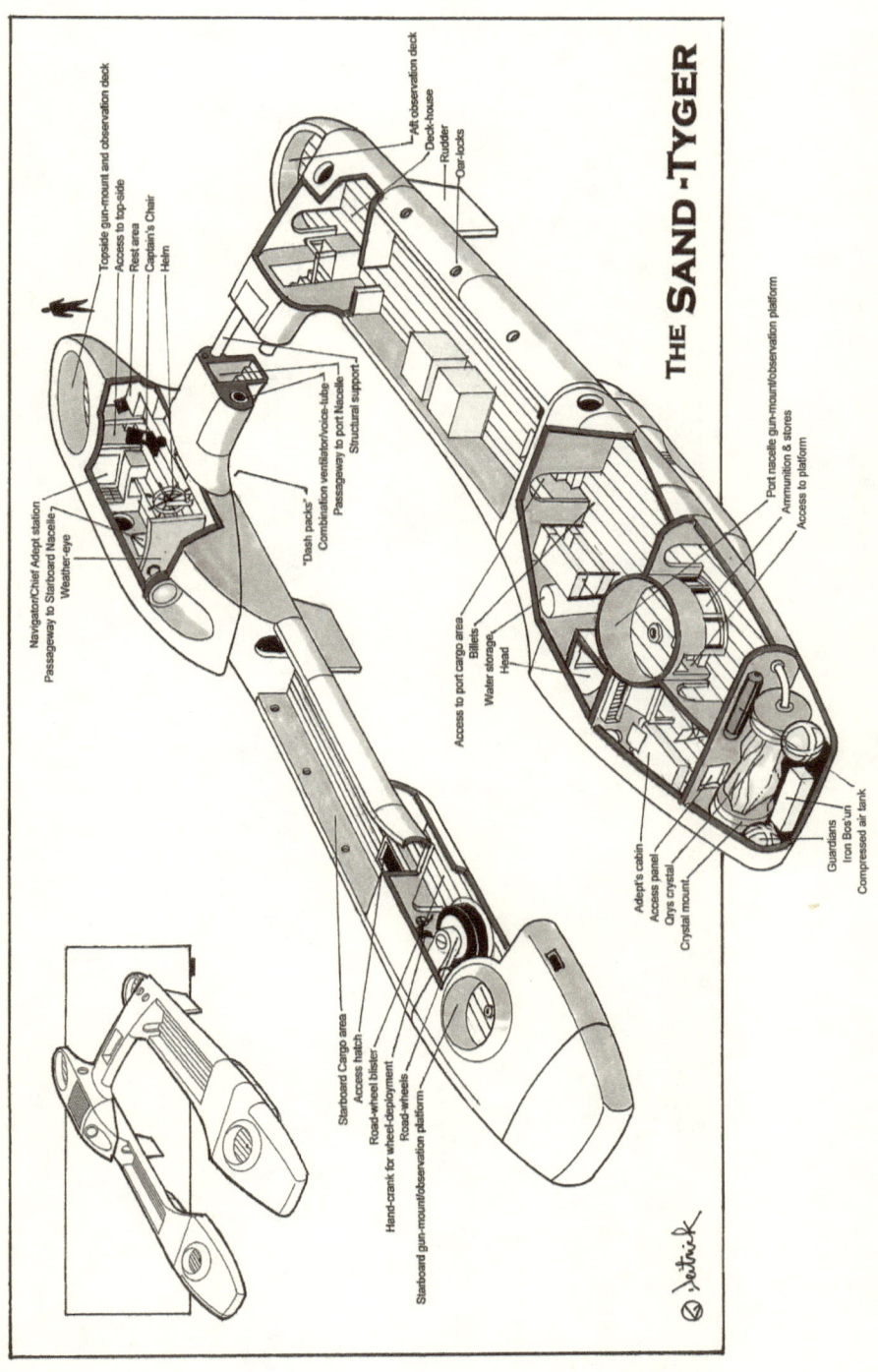

THE **SAND**-**TYGER**

Navigator/Chief Adept station
Passageway to Starboard Nacelle
Weather-eye

Topside gun-mount and observation deck
Access to top-side
Rest area
Captain's Chair
Helm

"Dash packs"
Combination ventilator/voice-tube
Passageway to port Nacelle
Structural support

Aft observation deck
Deck-house
Rudder
Oar-locks

Port nacelle gun-mount/observation platform
Ammunition & stores
Access to platform

Access to port cargo area
Billets
Water storage
Head

Adept's cabin
Access panel
Onyx crystal
Crystal mount

Guardians
Iron Bos'un
Compressed air tank

Starboard Cargo area
Access hatch
Road-wheel blister
Hand-crank for wheel-deployment
Road-wheels
Starboard gun-mount/observation platform

# CHAPTER ONE

## *SKYLLA*

*There's always been something lurking there beyond my minds-eye, but it wasn't until tonight I knew in my soul you were there…*

*Why have you come now, on this stormy night, and why do you still hide within the cloak of invisibility? You don't speak, and yet I feel your thoughts, your concerns, your yearning to know more about me…*

*Me… why me… a simple half-blood slave and freebooter trapped on a ship that is neither white-sailed sloop nor zeppelin but some amalgam in a world gone mad with petty dictators and burgeoning empires.*

*Stay then, if you will, but mind I don't take kindly to a touch or an unwanted advance. You stink of softness, of magic-void Samaya blood, and although I don't know how you've come to watch over me, I'll abide only what I'll abide, if you know what I mean…*

Rain pounded the deck, figures moving in the darkness with shuttered lamps. The Captain, Kaleb, stood still as a statue, water cascading off his wide-brimmed hat. He watched the darkness over the stern, his hands pressed against the rail.

From behind him the sanguine voice of Skylla cut through the downpour, "The storm is great cover, Captain."

She moved up beside Kaleb, her violet hair matted to her forehead and shoulders, her skin beaded with the night shower. The smell of the ocean was alive around her, the storm bringing forth her forbidden heritage even as her slave-bound oricalcum collar and bracers held it a bay.

"Yes, good cover… for them…" he replied.

She looked up at him, "Captain?"

He turned from the rail and marched across the deck, his boots splashing water as men stepped aside. With Skylla trailing after him, the Captain paused before entering the stern deckhouse, calling "Prepare for boarders!" over the sound of a booming thunderhead.

Skylla grabbed the nail-caster off her back and yelled to the crew, "Man battle stations!"

Men dropped the cargo they were hauling from the dock below the Sand-Tyger and raced aboard. A shot rang out, the final sailor up the gangplank shuddering as he fell off the ramp, his body splashing into the canal below.

Shouts came from the dock as men with bayoneted rifles swarmed out of the gloom, several pausing to take shots along the way. Another sailor screamed and pitched forward as Skylla raised her weapon and fired off two silver darts into the lead boarder.

From the port nacelle gun mount a cannon fired, the dock exploding in debris and men flying about. Two other sailors drew their short blades and engaged boarders at the gangplank. One received a bullet for his bravery, but the other slipped past a bayonet's thrust to drive his own blade into the throat of an enemy.

Skylla drew one of the two knives from the sheath at her thigh and ended another marauder's life with a quick toss to his head, the man pitching off the plank while two more took his place.

"Banished gods Kaleb! What are we hauling that would bring this?" she hissed.

A rifle round pinged off the nacelle to Skylla's right. She ducked, her nail-gun rising again to kill another boarder as he ran for the deckhouse. Light from the open door beyond the corpse dwindled as two sailors came forth with rifles in-hand.

Above, the cannon fired again, shaking the dock as debris peppered the side of the ship. Skylla cursed and pushed herself forward hydroplaning across the deck to the rail as she drew her last knife.

Shots rang out, more enemies screamed, but Skylla didn't look back to the combat's genesis point. Instead, leaning over the rail, she ran her knife across the thick hemp of a tether line. Her blade was made for throwing, but its double-edged steel was honed to a razors edge and she made quick work of the line.

The Sand-Tyger lurched sideways, the river current drawing the bow away from the dock. Another shot rang out, this one different from the bolt-rifles and the muskets. Skylla smiled as the ship's aft section pulled away from the dock.

"Great minds, Captain," she whispered.

As the Tyger broke away, the gangplank tumbled down into the canal and took four of the enemy with it.

Turning, Skylla raised her weapon and fired another dart, this one taking a marauder in the neck, his three companions throwing down their weapons before leaping over the rail as the remainder of the crew closed in with blades in hand.

"Tormay!" Skylla yelled, "Do you have to fire that saint's-damned cannon every time we see combat?"

A man with long mustache beneath his leather aviator's hat and goggles leaned over the nacelle to smile down at her.

He pointed to his left ear, "What? I can't hear ya!"

The deck lurched again, this time the ship rising in the water and straightening out. Skylla looked back to the bridge, but the contained section between the command node the starboard pontoon revealed no inner mystery.

"Laramy!" she called.

"Dead, Miss," Parish yelled back.

"Olaf?" she asked.

"Here!" a thickly accented voice sounded above the rain from the port deckhouse door.

"Get this cargo secured, and if anyone's hurt get them out of the rain," she said.

Olaf nodded, joined by a lean man who moved out into the downpour while buttoning a white slicker at the shoulder.

"Wounded?" the man asked.

Skylla moved up the deck, kicked a discarded musket from her path, and then looked over the damage at the genesis. Three men were down, all dead and all marauders. A forth was leaning against the rail with his hands clutching his left arm.

"Here doc," she called. "It's Stoneham."

The doctor moved over to the man, and Skylla left him to his business as she continued to shout orders. The storm dumped its fury in sheets as the Tyger picked up speed. Olaf, the bosun's mate – thick as an ox and with arms round as a strong man's thigh – echoed her commands until she slipped into the port deckhouse, trusting him to know what needed to be done.

Sighing, she leaned her back against the cool metal of a bulkhead and closed her eyes.

"Rough night?" a voice asked.

Her thigh-blade was out and at the speaker's throat before he could blink. Eyes focusing, she swore and withdrew the blade.

"Ryan Ugarth, you're going to die sneaking up on people like that," she hissed.

Ugarth, fair-haired and pretty as a Findalynn dandy, rubbed his hand over his throat and smiled, saying, "It would be worth it if the hand that dealt the blow was yours."

"You better find a more believable line than that next time you broker a deal for Kaleb or it will certainly be your last," she said.

He put a hand over his breast, "You wound me more than any blow, dear lady."

Her eyes flashed emerald and the smell of the ocean filled the room, "Slaves aren't ladies, Ugarth, so if you want to charm me to your bed you should be pouring honey in the captain's ear, not mine."

He tipped his head as she pushed past him, her boots clanking against the stair leading to the command node.

The tight quarters of the stair opened into the larger bridge. Skylla noted that Kaleb was absent, and Arvilla was seated in this captain's chair, her dark eyes focused on the weather-eye. The navigator was a chocolate-skinned Hilani with a wasp waist, hair rowed and braided, and as tall as any man among the crew.

"Where's the captain?" Skylla asked.

"He went starboard looking for Pascal. We lose anyone?"

Skylla walked past her. Morgan, the young wheelman, turned the helm to port but didn't join the conversation.

"We lost Laramy, Kolb, and Renni… not sure about Stoneham. The doc is working on him."

"Captain won't be happy," Arvilla said.

Skylla started down the stair, "When is he ever happy?"

A laugh followed her down to the starboard deckhouse, the smell of perfume and spice drifting up into the stair and a pale green smoke lingering in the damp of the storm. The deckhouse held two doors, one forward and one aft, but the bulk of the chamber was hung with thick tapestries of wool and silk. Brass braziers, cushions, and Ushan-inspired demi-saint sculptures decorated the room.

"Skylla, is that you?" a woman's voice called from behind the curtains.

Skylla didn't reply, instead slipping sideways to the starboard deck door and back out into the driving rain.

"Saint's curses, this storm won't end soon enough for me," she hissed.

Branson, a stout northerner with blonde hair swept back in a braid, stood sentry at the starboard billets hatch.

"Captain in there?" she asked.

He nodded, rain flowing down his hawkish nose in a stream. She threw the latch and opened the door. Inside the air was cool with lanterns burning low and the smell of oil thick in the air.

"What's the report?" Kaleb called from further back.

She made her way through the room, finger running over the ceiling to help guide her until she saw the captain kneeling next to the legs of Pascal, who was obscured by a huge wheel.

"Three dead, one wounded, doc's having a look," she said.

Kaleb nodded, then asked, "The cargo?"

"Secure, sir, but can I ask what that was all about at the docks?"

Rising, Kaleb stretched his back with a loud pop, then took a breath.

"How much longer?" he asked.

Pascal's feet twitched, "Another thirty minutes and I'll have the wheels ready."

"Good, let me know as soon as you do because we've got to stay with the storm or the crossing won't matter."

Pascal said something that was lost in the metalwork, and Kaleb stepped up beside Skylla, his finger coming up to brush his thick mustache.

"What's say we take a walk on the deck and I tell you a secret," he said.

"You know it's raining, right?"

He smiled, "I thought water-born liked the rain?"

Her expression soured, but she nodded and went with him, the duo disappearing into the driving shower outside the door.

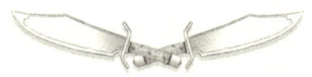

# CHAPTER TWO

## *KALEB*

*I sense you're here again, lurking in the haze of my mind like a dull headache. No matter, what's done is done and I can't take it back now.*

*I have no true defense as I'm just a man charged with the well -being of his crew. We need money, we need parts, and we need food... those are the facts of life that stare back at me with dead eyes each day from my stateroom mirror.*

*Did you see my three men die? Two had families, one was newly married, and now I've got to send a post by some rogue trader and hope it finds them. Did you hear that? I have to hope a note telling someone their father, their love, their husband is dead and won't be coming back.*

*That's the type of world we live in... that is the Gun Kingdoms, and now I also have you to contend with, you who steals into my dreams and lurks in shadows as I pass in the daylight.*

*Follow then, as I seem unable to dissuade you, but make no mistake. I've got business to attend and any interference will be dealt with most harshly...*

Rain continued down in blinding sheets, and the river was an oily black serpent beneath the rail as the Sand-Tyger cut along the water's surface.

Kaleb stood next to Skylla, his first mate barely reaching his shoulder even with her boots' heels, two figures set against the dark canopy of night and well out of earshot of the sentry.

"How many boxes did we get on board?" he asked.

"Eleven before the attack came," she replied.

He nodded, "Good, that will at least confuse them for the moment."

"Captain, again, what was in those boxes?"

"What do you know of the War of Bone and Steel?" he asked in reply.

Skylla shook her head, "That it was long ago, a century at least, and that the tales insist it was the end of my kind."

"Yes, but the greatest secret of that war is that the Samaya used magic to destroy the Enlightened, burning the races of the Shining Cities with the very elements that gave them power over us."

"Captain?"

He looked down at her, water pouring off his hat. "Once the conflict ended, the Samaya alliances broke apart and the people destroyed the same tome mages who had helped them win the war. My people turned their backs on magic, just as they rejected ships like the Sand-Tyger, but that doesn't mean other relics like this one don't still exist."

Skylla turned, her eyes scanning the boxes in the port pontoon.

Kaleb said, "One, and only one, of those boxes we brought on board holds elemental cores, fire-cores to be precise, and there are powers in the world that will still pay a king's ransom for access to them."

She looked back at him, hair slick and honeyed-skin beaded with water. The cold of the night didn't touch her, the Enlightened blood in her veins at home in its own element.

"Captain, are they dangerous?" she asked.

"Only if kept away from water, otherwise they're stable."

"Then we're to go to sea?"

He shook his head, "No, the Halo crawls with frigates and a blockade exists in the Horned Straights where the Garin Clans keep the Free City of Tiefon locked away from the rest of the world."

She looked back to the cargo, "Do I want to know?"

He laughed, "You'll need to know because I'm going to have to have every bit of your guile to pull this off."

"You're planning on going across the continent…"

"See, you're already smarter than the bulk of all the free captains on the Halo," he said.

"And twice as foolish I think," she began. "There's no way you can keep the Tyger on water the whole time."

Pascal called from the starboard billets, "Captain, she's ready!"

Kaleb smiled down at Skylla, "I can, and I will…"

The Tyger lurched, Skylla grabbing a bulkhead and Kaleb clutching the armrests of his command chair. Ahead the weather-eye displayed the ground in front of the Tyger's twin pontoons, crewmen with unshuttered lanterns leading a path over a waterlogged and grassy rise from the river-bank.

"Keep her steady Mr. Gates," Kaleb said.

The young wheelman, Morgan Gates, fought with the wheel, but the Tyger kept her course, the men leading the way up and over the first rise.

"Time?" Kaleb asked.

"Second Moon, third hour and eighth minute," Arvilla answered.

Kaleb nodded, his eyes fixed on the viewer. "Skylla, how's the storm?"

Skylla closed her eyes and after a moment answered, "It's blowing out, maybe an hour or two left in her."

"Which is it, an hour or two?" he asked.

She opened her eyes, fingers twining over the silvered bands at her arms, her lips tight, "Two if the wind holds."

Turning to his left, Kaleb leaned over and spoke into the conical opening of a brass tube attached to his chair.

"I'm going to need more speed Pascal."

From the tube, a distant voice slithered out, "You can go to ten REMs, but if you hit something at that speed it's not my fault when she breaks down."

Kaleb nodded, "You hear that Mr. Gates? Don't hit anything."

"Aye, sir." Morgan replied.

Kaleb leaned to the tube again, "Make it ten REMs."

The ship jumped, Skylla holding on while a map and several silver instruments fell from Arvilla's navigation table. Ahead, the viewer showed the lantern's swinging wildly as men ran out of the ship's way.

Kaleb leaned to a second tube, this one on the right of his chair, "Come aboard gentlemen, we're going to full drive."

Outside, the captain's words were echoed across the decks. The lanterns disappeared, two huge lights blazing to life on each of the pontoon bow nacelles. The Tyger lumbered over the landscape, the river falling away in the distance as it cut across the open grassland toward the south.

Kaleb listened to the ship shudder, moan, and grind for over an hour, the rains settling into a misty shower as amber light stole the pitch from the clouds above and replaced it with tumbling grey curves.

"Arvilla, how long?" he asked.

"At this speed, thirty minutes," she said.

He shook his head and then leaned into the left tube. "Pascal, I'm going to need fifteen."

"The wheels aren't checked for that," Pascal reported.

"Fifteen Pascal," Kaleb repeated.

The Tyger started to shake, the landscape – now illuminated by the growing dawn – drifting past like shades in the mist.

"Skylla, take over for Mr. Gates," Kaleb ordered.

Gates stifled a protest. His eyes red and his knuckles white, he gave the helm to Skylla without argument.

"Good work, Mr. Gates. Now head up to the lamps and tell the spotters to keep us clear of the big stuff," Kaleb commanded.

Morgan saluted and then left the bridge by way of the port stair. From the starboard stair, a thin figure appeared dressed in a cape of midnight silk, face and head cloaked in a black lace veil.

"Captain, the starboard pontoon is shuddering like a naked man on a block of ice," the newcomer said.

Her voice was thin and raspy but with a hint of youth, and she braced herself against a bulkhead. Her pale hand was covered in a henna scrawl that tangled back to a ringed copper bracer that was identical to Skylla's oricalcum set.

"I'm aware of the ship's condition, Mya, now clear the bridge," Kaleb said.

Mya nodded, turned, and then hesitated, saying, "Master Laramy was on my schedule for this evening but he's failed to appear."

"He's dead, you've the evening to yourself," Kaleb replied.

"Will the captain then partake?" she asked.

Kaleb, face flushed and eyes hard turned from the weather-eye, "Clear the bridge!"

She slipped away and Kaleb returned to the viewer, his fingers tapping the brass studs on the leather armrest before he finally started to suck at his front teeth. Minutes passed, the sun breaking the dawn and the rain giving way to a layer of fine mist.

"There!" Skylla called.

Kaleb fell back into his chair, "I see it, mark a course."

Skylla adjusted the helm, the Tyger turned until the viewer displayed the ghost-tangled waters of a lake steaming in the morning air.

Kaleb sighed and leaned into the left tube, "Prepare for splashdown, Pascal, we're almost home."

The Sand-Tyger slipped across the smooth surface of Arabel Lake, the tumbledown hills and thick forests of the interior counties of Dragmarsh far off to the east and south. Kaleb let the early spring wind burn his cheeks as he sat in the gunner's seat in the aft nacelle, just above the command cluster.

The Captain was alone, while some of the crew labored on menial tasks in the pontoons below, and he took a deep breath before gaining his feet and heading for the stairs. The bridge was clear save for Morgan, who once again held the helm. Kaleb gave the kid a nod before heading down the starboard stair to the deckhouse below.

"Mya," he called.

Curtains shifted in the back half of the room, the dark-clad Gola coming out as she attached her veil to a clip on the left side of her cloak.

"Yes, captain?"

"May I come in?" he asked.

She nodded and pushed a curtain aside, the smell of incense strong beyond the fabric wall. He slipped inside the room, more a sun-strider's tent than a ship's compartment. The only true furnishing was a low wide bed that held sumptuous sheets and no pillows.

"What can I do for you captain?" she asked.

He took a seat among floor cushions as Mya did the same. All her cloaks concealed every inch of flesh save for her fingers and eyes.

"I wanted to apologize for this morning on the bridge," he said.

Her eyes narrowed. "You need not apologize to your Gola, captain. I'm a servant, a slave, and I require no words of apology."

"You are indeed my Gola, but you bring luck to the ship and crew and I find it distasteful to draw ire against you without true provocation," he said.

"It's always honor with you Captain, a strange thing in this hedonistic and immoral world, and especially in the lawless fringes in which you dwell."

He nodded, "Nevertheless, I'm sorry, and I want you to adjust your books to the absence of Masters Kolb, Renni, as well as Laramy."

"I shall do so…"

He rose to his feet but she stayed him with a word, "Captain?"

"Yes?"

"I was to paramour Renni this evening, and my virtues will go to Olaf unless you have an objection."

Kaleb shook his head, "Why would I?"

She rose next to him, her eyes blue as sapphires and almost on level with his. "You could take his place with me, let me bring my luck to you as is proper among the very nature and purpose of all Gola."

Her fingers reached to touch him, but he backed a step away. "No, I respect your place, but you know I cannot."

"A man was not meant to hold what you do, thrice the burden of any on this ship, and yet you take no release. It is an improper thing..."

Kaleb shook his head, "I'm an Academy man..."

She cut him off, "Academy men created the Gola, so that is no excuse."

"Mya, Olaf needs to be moved up. We'll be in Findalynn in two days. Put that in the books and collect all the fallen men's things for dispersal among wives and family. Understood?"

She nodded and he stepped through the curtain, causing Skylla to take a quick step back on the far side. He stared at her a moment, her left foot finally sliding behind her right as she gave an innocent smile.

"Captain," she said.

"Skylla"

He moved past her, his boots ringing on the steps up to the command node. Behind him the quiet hiss of women's voices drifted up the stair.

# CHAPTER THREE

## *SKYLLA*

*I*t's both pretty and ugly isn't it? Findalynn, former Shining City and now home to almost half a million Samaya.

They say that it was once an Enlightened stronghold, that my people lived here like immortal Gods but now it's little more than a place of commerce and darkness.

See the spires, those like the upturned legs of a dead spider? They were magic born, forged of fabled oricalcum and etched with saintly magic no streambender could overturn. Now they lay dark and dead as the dreams of my kind...

This new city, holding Samaya like rats among the ruins, sprawls out among the feted canals once so grand and clean that folk could swim among fish golden and white like the petals of spring flowers. It is no more, and yet I must come here as I always do, back to the slave platforms, dead eyes, and hungry mouths I knew as a youth...

You would come too? Then you have more stomach than I would have thought, but no matter, I stand beside my captain, the man who saved me from this place, and with him I am protected...

The plank fell into place, Olaf smiling a gap-toothed grin as he bowed to her like royalty, his hand waving out toward the docks.

"After you," he said.

Skylla didn't comment, but stepped aside as Kaleb and Ugarth walked past, Olaf grabbing his tattered hat off his head and saluting.

"Captain!" he said.

Kaleb didn't stop, saying, "See that no one comes aboard. We won't be long."

Olaf nodded and Skylla shot him a dark look as she followed both men down the plank. When they reached the bottom Kaleb turned to Ugarth and adjusted his hat. "I don't need trouble, Mr. Ugarth, so keep the dock-master off our backs until I get back, understood?"

Ugarth nodded, "That's my job."

Kaleb grunted and then walked away with Skylla close at his heels. The streets were dark cobbles set with heavy pavers where hasty repairs had taken place over the years. Buildings lining the docks were in similar disrepair, as heavy stone walls were patched with wood, thatch, and mortar.

People milled about in homespun browns and whites with a spot of black thrown in here and there for added color. Dirty faces, unkempt hair, and the smell of the unclean filled the avenue. The sounds of dock workers calling from riverboats clashed against clattering carriages and hoarse-voiced venders as Kaleb turned down a thin alley and made his way to the next block in.

"You watch my back," he said.

"Always," she replied.

They crossed a street, a horse and rider meandering past and a woman in a black dress and parasol casting them a suspicious eye as the two men flanking her slipped hands inside their coats. The moment of tension passed, the woman continuing on as Kaleb crossed another intersection and took a second alley. This one twisted back like a serpent, buildings on either side looming over the thin passage. The smell of feces clung heavy in the damp air.

Skylla let her hand drop to her knife sheath, the twin hilts at her thigh playing against her fingertips.

"*This is a nasty business, captain… and I hate coming down to Shay's Circle,*" she whispered.

The tangle of buildings finally gave way to a twisted iron gate, rusted and hanging ajar. When Kaleb touched it a piercing screech of metal against metal sent the hair on Skylla's neck at attention.

New sounds rippled through the courtyard beyond as though buildings awoke, and a pipe was struck somewhere, the reverberation echoing among the shuttered windows above.

"Captain?" she asked.

He moved forward, boots crunching yellow grass amid the cracked pavers of the square. She watched the windows above: a twitch of movement here, a shade pulled closed there, but nothing else visible. A Mourning Crow squawked from a roof, its white form looking like the ghost of an imp as it hopped along a broken gutter.

*A bad sign, that...*

They came to a two story building on the far side of the court, the stone pitted and stained with white streaks, and a layer of coal dust hanging on every horizontal surface. A window with scrawling letters painted on it read 'Abab's Emporium', and beside it a scarlet painted door stood out like a lady among whores with its bright lacquer and polished brass fittings.

Kaleb entered, a bell sounding above the door frame. The interior was warm, a stove in the middle of the main room providing heat and an iron pot atop it whistled with steam. Around the stove a collection of circular bookcases moved out to the walls, each oddly spaced to make it impossible to see further back than a single aisle. The shelves were lined with all manner of tomes, bottles, jars, and trinkets. Rectangular, yellowed tags attached with green ribbons were fastened to most.

"Who enters?" a voice thick with the flavors of the Pagan Coast drifted out of the stacks.

"You know full well, but you always ask," Kaleb responded.

A laugh followed, then the sound of a mechanical lever falling back into place. Kaleb looked at Skylla, and she surreptitiously drew her fingers away from her knives.

A man appeared, thin as a cane pole and brown as old leather. He wore black silk trousers, crimson slippers, and a fine cotton coat with brass flares that were buttoned all the way up this neck. A small tasseled hat decorated his bald head, wisps of smoky hair lingering around his ears, one of which was cut short by a blade at some point in his past.

"Kaleb! What brings an old friend to my shop?" the man asked.

He stepped forward and embraced the Captain, the two patting each other on the back before the shop keeper fell back and cast his amber eyes on Skylla.

"And who is this?" he asked.

"Abab Drask, this is my first mate, Skylla," Kaleb said.

Drask reached out and took her hand, his wrinkled fingers trailing over the lines in her palms.

"A new one again? It seems you're always in need of first mates my friend..."

Kaleb nodded, his hand going out to touch a skull with three tiny horn-nubs on the crown. Abab's smile faded and he coughed, let go Skylla's hand, and moved to take the skull from the shelf.

"Touch only what you intend to buy, my friend, you know this."

"My apologies. Rules about touching are sometimes easily forgotten, no?" Kaleb asked innocently.

Abab stared at him a moment, chuckled, and then nodded as he retreated back into the stacks.

"Indeed... indeed..."

Kaleb followed, Skylla staying close.

"So, I ask again, what's brought you today?"

"The season, I'd heard the Isle of Bringe has no more snow even this early," Kaleb answered.

Abab stopped but didn't look back, saying, "Snow came not to Bringe this year, or hadn't you heard?"

"I hadn't, my season was spent in Taux," Kaleb replied.

Abab nodded and then slid between two stacks disappearing. Skylla moved close to Kaleb, whispering, "What's this about?"

"What do you think?"

She sighed, *the damnable cargo...*

A few minutes passed as Kaleb wandered among the stacks, sometimes leaning in for a closer look but never touching the wares.

Abab appeared as suddenly as he'd exited, a rolled parchment and a folded piece of paper in his hands. Behind him stood a youth with sandy-blonde hair. His face was marked with red blemishes. He was taller than Kaleb, and nearly as wide.

"Your package arrived yesterday, but it's my hope you'll leave it and I can tell those interested you never came by," Abab proclaimed.

"It's too late for that and you know it, my friend, but I take your words with the favor in which they were meant."

Abab sighed and then handed over the items. "Very well, but I would know if you have positions open on the Tyger. This youth has been working for me since his parents died of the Ashen Eye, but I've little use for someone of his size in a shop like this."

Kaleb looked the young man over. "What's your name?"

"Yogo, sir," he answered.

"He's a hard worker, albeit clumsy at his age. Still growing I think," Abab said.

Nodding, the Captain slipped the papers into his jacket, "I'll take him on your recommendation, but you know as well as I he'll probably not last the year."

Abab shrugged, "Life is fickle, but his lines are strong, much like those of your new first mate."

Frowning, Kaleb turned toward the door, "Very well."

Abab's voice trailed behind, "Remember, Yogo, do as those on the crew tell you, especially the captain!" This was, apparently, all the farewell the new crew member would receive.

The bell chimed, and the exterior courtyard had slipped into shadow as the sun dipped slowly west. Coal smoke rose from the upper stories, the air was thick with it, and the gloom of the place was tenfold what it had been when they'd entered.

The newly-formed trio retraced their steps, but when they reached the gate it was closed, a chain thrown around the bars that linked it to the stone of an adjoining building. Above laughter drifted down in the haze, and Skylla drew a knife...

She made a keen throw, and the man running toward her pitched forward with a gurgle as two more took his place. Beside her Kaleb drew a gladius from beneath his trench, the weapon's edge turning a blow from a pipe as another man came from their flank.

"Saint's alive, I love Shay's Circle," Skylla hissed.

A man grabbed at her but she dodged under his arms, pulling her momentum through to her knee as it impacted with his groin. The man fell, but another attacker caught Skylla from behind. Throwing back her head, her skull connected with his face and he released her.

Skylla spun, struck out with her right foot and sent him tumbling back into the gate. Beside her Yogo was wrestling with another man. The attacker started biting the kid's upper arm until Yogo let out a scream and released him.

Skylla drew her second knife, turned, and threw again. Her blade drove smoothly into the eye of an assailant trying to flank the Captain.

The blinded man let out a scream, flopping backward with legs still kicking. Kaleb's blade slipped past his attacker's metal pipe and opened him at the waist, blood splattering the stones at his feet before he fell next to Skylla's victim.

She nodded and turned, the gate crasher having recovered enough to jump at her again. This time she sidestepped his lunge and reversed her field to give him an elbow to his already bloody nose. The impact shattered his face, eyes turning in, as his legs gave out as he fell forward like a marionette without strings.

Another scream came from the ground. Yogo had gained the upper hand by putting his thumbs into his attacker's eyes and pushing them with all his weight into the unfortunate man's skull.

And yet, the fight was not finished. Three more men came from a door twenty paces away, clubs in hand. Before the trio could react, the leading man among the newcomers dropped dead as a shot rang out.

Kaleb stood with his pistol raised, smoke rising from the barrel, and the other men dropped their weapons as they backed into the building.

"Yogo," Skylla said.

The boy was still crushing the corpse, his thumbs fully sunk as blood covered his hands like red satin gloves.

"Yogo!"

The boy shook his head, finally turning as he slowly pulled his hands free with a sucking sound.

"I…" he whispered.

She pulled him up by his shoulder, the boy's hands shaking and blood dripping down from the bite wound in his right arm.

"Hard first day on the job… but I've seen worse, so be thankful," she said.

Yogo nodded dumbly as he held his hands away from his body, staring. Behind her the first attacker was still choking and trying to rise as he clutched his groin with one hand. She watched as Kaleb approached him, pistol going out until it touched the man's temple.

He froze, one hand going up. "Please…" he whispered.

"Get up," the Captain ordered.

The man staggered to his feet, a mop of dirty black hair hanging over his pale face. Skylla went to retrieve her knives, while Kaleb walked in front of the last attacker using the pistol's barrel to move the hair from in front of the man's face.

"How old are you?" Kaleb asked.

Skylla looked up as she withdrew her knife from a corpse's eye. The final attacker was thin, with pronounced cheekbones and eyes as blue as the equatorial ocean. His skin was as flawless as Yogo's was tragic, and although sunken-eyed, he was handsome with a bit of stubble clinging to his chin and upper lip that hadn't yet completed the journey to a full beard.

"I… I don't know…" he said.

"Can you read?" Kaleb asked.

"No…"

"Show me your teeth."

The young man provided a wan smile. His teeth were all there, the gums and edging a bit grey.

Kaleb released the pistol's hammer with his thumb, saying, "I lost three crewmen this week and I need replacements. You interested in joining a crew?"

The man's eyes bulged, "What?"

"I'd give a better answer than that. He won't ask twice," Skylla said.

The youth shook his head, "Uh…"

Kaleb holstered his pistol and looked at Skylla, "Keys?"

She lifted a single iron skeleton from a corpse and smiled.

"Let's get out of here before this crew finds their balls or worse yet the constables make an appearance," he said.

Skylla ran to the gate and slipped the key into the lock. The device gave and she pulled the chain free, the sound echoing in the courtyard and she hissed a curse.

Behind her Kaleb placed a hand on Yogo's shoulder. "You did well, kid, and I'm sorry to say this will never leave you, that feeling you have after killing a man so close. It's personal, but remember, it could be you lying there, so never regret it."

Yogo nodded, but said nothing. Kaleb pulled a handkerchief from his coat and handed it to him.

"Clean up, those hands would draw too much attention on the way back to the Tyger as they are," he said.

Skylla pulled the gate open and Kaleb helped Yogo through, the two disappearing down the dark alley. Skylla looked back, a thin smile crossing her face.

"You coming?" she asked.

The sole surviving attacker, hands still raised, blinked, looked around him at his dead compatriots, and then shuffled toward the gate with pained grunts. She stopped him before he could move past her, a hand on his chest.

"The captain is a kind man, forgiving to a flaw, but if you cross him and he doesn't kill you first, I will… understood?"

The man nodded.

"What's your name?"

"Greylin Sumner… but my friends just call me Grey," he answered.

"Well, Greylin, welcome aboard the Sand-Tyger."

# CHAPTER FOUR

## *KALEB*

*I can almost feel the judgment, but I contend I've a better perspective than you. I learned long ago that the keys to a person's soul are in their eyes. I've seen madness in them, anger, and yes, even evil, but once you can discern the truth from them you can establish trust.*

*That boy was a product of his environment, much like Skylla or any other member of my crew. When I got a look in his eyes I instantly knew his story. He can be trusted, more so now than at any other time in his life because of the gift I've given him: freedom of choice.*

*This is the way I operate, and if you don't see the value in it then I invite you to move along to other men because I still have no use for you and your spying eyes…*

Stoneham leaned against the rail next to Kaleb, the quartermaster naked above the waist save for several tattoos and a linen bandage wrapped around his arm..

"They look like fools." Stoneham observed.

Kaleb smiled and sucked hard on a cigar, the smoke easing his mind as he watched the youngest members of the crew running like angry ants over the beach. The darkness of Findalynn lay two days to the north, and the southern turn of the Dragmarsh coast was a place of gentle trades, warm southern currents, and unspoiled wilderness.

"They need the exercise, life on a ship can wear out your legs," Kaleb replied.

Stoneham harrumphed and then called an insult to the boys on the beach, his hand pointing south. Morgan, Parish, Yogo, and Greylin were all in their knickers, wet with sea-spray and carrying nets and spears like archipelago islanders.

"They'll never catch one," Stoneham said.

"They better or this trip will be a lot shorter than I had planned," Kaleb said.

Stoneham turned to him. The ship's officer wore a set of chops that framed a cut chin, his hair orange and flecked with gold. "Do I even want to know why?"

Kaleb took another long draw on the cigar and said nothing. On the beach, Morgan was shouting, Yogo having tripped into the surf with Greylin poking at large brush with his spear while Parish held his net out on the far side.

"I thought it was strange you had a hankering for Glagaas. The birds aren't known as a delicacy in any port I've ever made call," Stoneham said.

"I'll not be the one having a feast, my friend," Kaleb answered.

The Captain then turned to the port nacelle and pointed to the shore. Tormay waved and pulled the cord on his cannon. The sound echoed in the bay, sea birds taking flight all over the trees. The bush Greylin was poking exploded with Glagaas, the ground birds – each the size of a large house cat – skittering out in a mass of grey feathers, long beaks, and white legs.

On the nacelle Tormay started hooting and hollering as Parish was quickly overcome with fleeing birds. Yogo, in a panic as the spent round impacted in the forest, started swimming for the Tyger. Morgan took cover among some nearby boulders.

Greylin ducked, took two steps around the bush, and then speared a Glagaas that had changed direction away from Parish's net. The bird went limp and their newest crew member raised a fist in triumph as he looked toward the ship.

"Damned lucky, that," Stoneham said.

Kaleb smiled and pointed to the bush where Parish struggled to contain another three Glagaas that had gotten their webbed feet caught in his net. "No, Parish's mighty catch is lucky."

Waving first to Greylin, Kaleb then turned and gave Tormay a thumbs up and walked off the cargo deck.

The Tyger cut a path down the coast, the tranquil shore south of Findalynn growing wild, dark, and tangled as the ship finally made it to the Dragmarsh Delta, a place of swamps and tributaries that sucked down both men and ships alike.

Kaleb watched from the command nacelle, arms resting on the smooth wood of the circular rail that surrounded the observation platform. Crewmen Parish and Greylin sat on the front of the port and starboard pontoons, twenty-foot poles balanced across their thighs, their duty a reward for the success of their hunt the day before.

From behind Kaleb's position Doc Rose muttered, "I'll say it if she won't, this is insanity Captain."

The older gentleman, with his coat nicely buttoned and his short grey hair trimmed as cleanly as his beard, stood a few paces away rubbing a handkerchief over his rectangular spectacles. Skylla stood beside the doctor, her normally near naked body covered with a rain slicker as the breeze carried a chill from the coming dawn.

"You know, Doc, you're rarely wrong, but that doesn't mean we're not going in there," Kaleb said.

"Oh, I know, but at least someone has to talk reason when no one else will," Rose said.

Kaleb chuckled, "I guess that's why a freeman such as yourself, who joined the crew without my request, is a good thing to have aboard. Otherwise I'd be stuck with a gaggle of saluting drones, right Skylla?"

His First Officer simply stared at him. Rose put a hand on her shoulder, saying, "He's as passive aggressive as his father. Don't let it get to you my dear."

Kaleb leaned over the rail to get a look at the port cargo deck. Branson stood guard over the freight, a rifle in hand and hussars cap pulled down over his eyes.

"Skylla."

"Captain?"

"Get the poles up and ready, I'm taking the helm."

"Yes Captain."

Kaleb moved back down the stair, while Arvilla slipped from the command chair before he could get there.

"Thanks for warming it," the Captain said.

The woman didn't reply as she took her place at the navigator's desk.

"What say you, Mr. Gates, any chance you'll be running us aground today?" Kaleb asked.

"No sir, you can trust my skills," Morgan replied.

Kaleb smiled and then turned to Arvilla, "Do the maps work for you?"

"As much as any can, but Captain, you know this delta is constantly moving. By the Saints, the storm we went through last week was enough to change several courses, and I've no idea how fresh this map even is."

"That's why I've brought the Glagass," he said.

"Captain?" she asked, raising an eyebrow.

"Just take us into the tidewaters and keep to the pirate signs, I'll handle the rest," he said.

"What about Ja'kraaft? Are you planning on making call there?" she asked.

"I'm known in the stronghold, so is Mr. Ugarth, which should be enough to get us in if we have to make landfall, but it's my hope that won't be necessary."

Arvilla said no more and Kaleb leaned into the tube to his right, saying, "Pascal, take us to 5 REM."

The ship slid across the waves, the weather-eye showing the front of the vessel as Parish and Greylin got to their feet, poles at the ready. The water was muddy and the tides were high as Arvilla called out the route and Gates shifted the helm.

Kaleb watched the shore move ever closer, the trees a mix of tangled vines and broad-leaf ikola that clung to the mud and rocks at the water's edge while fern and flowing locas became an impenetrable wall beneath.

The Tyger slipped past the dozen watery mouths of the tidewater, twenty minutes of slow going followed before the poles were extended as the ship reached the first cataract. Boulders lifted yellow molded faces from the water, and swirls of white-water tangled around submerged brothers to the exposed mustard-clad ancients.

"Steady, Mr. Gates, watch the poles, they'll give you a sign if need be." Kaleb said.

He leaned over again, speaking into the conical, "Drop us to 2 REM, Pascal."

The ship crept on, the poles moving out and Morgan adjusting course several times over an hour's span before the water opened up to a more tranquil span. Kaleb let out a sigh, stood and stretched, saying, "Well done, Mr. Gates, now see us through this river, and in another two hours we'll be to the first lake."

Kaleb moved back toward the chair, his eye catching those of Arvilla, "You have the helm."

She nodded, answering routinely, "I have the helm" as the Captain went back up the steps. Doc Rose and Skylla were still in the nacelle. Rose sat in a wooden folding chair snoring quietly and Skylla had shed her trench, her honey skin taking on a warm ruddy complexion as she leaned against the front rail.

*Saints… she'll be the death of me.*

Kaleb looked past her exposed hindquarters and made his way to the rail beside her. A collection of long-legged white fishers trolled the banks to the starboard pontoon, and two pale, pink, Torga's dolphins played in the wake of the port. Parish and Greylin were watching them as they took a rest.

"A nice day," Kaleb observed softly.

Skylla turned, her violet hair falling down over her left eye before she tucked it behind her ear.

"Why captain, I didn't know you noticed such things," she said.

He chuckled, "Am I that gruff?"

"Yes…" Rose mumbled and then went back to snoring.

Kaleb shook his head and Skylla turned back to the river. Absently, she clicked her silvered left bracer against the rail.

"They say this delta can't be navigated and even pirates who grew up here their whole lives never travel north of Ja'kraaft," she said.

"That's true, but then again I'm no pirate."

She smiled, but hid it with her hand.

"You're the strangest man I've ever met… and that's saying something because I'm a slaveborn," she said.

He looked at her, half naked with only a white harem skirt and breast wrap to conceal her most intimate parts. She wore high brown boots with heavy heels, and her only other decoration were the oricalcum bracers and neck-ring, all plated and cast with subtle runes.

"This criticism from my First Mate who dresses for a Findalynn brothel when she can wear anything she likes," Kaleb said.

She shrugged, "Why hide what I am? Would you have me be different?"

Their eyes met, hers dark and emerald and his amber flecked with gold. They stared a long moment until she finally looked away. His hand flexed as if to reach for her but she turned and slipped down the stair to the bridge below.

"Stupid as always." Doc whispered.

Kaleb turned on the elder man as the physician stood and slid his coat back over his shoulders.

"How can you sleep and still hear everything?" Kaleb asked.

"It's the secret of my success, just ask any of my old professors at the Surgeon's Guild."

Shaking his head, Kaleb looked back at the river, "You know I'm ten years her elder."

"Stupid," Doc replied.

"She's a slave," Kaleb said.

"Stupid," Doc echoed.

"I'm an aristocrat."

"Stupid."

Kaleb turned, "Stop saying that!"

The doctor put on his glasses and smiled, "If I don't say it, who will? Stop saying stupid things, and I won't have to say it again."

They stared at each other until Parish started calling from the port pontoon as the ship turned to starboard.

"I'll be in my quarters if needed," Rose said.

The doctor ambled down the steps and Kaleb looked back at the river, the shadow of a sandbar clear from his vantage.

*Well done, Mr. Parish... you've saved us some trouble.*

The Tyger moved on, Kaleb staying atop the nacelle as the sun crept slowly across the sky.

The ghost moon hung close over the waters of the lake, its reflection illuminating the surface as its smaller bloody sister hung back, the crimson glow kept in check by its larger sibling in the early night.

Kaleb stood on the port cargo rail, holding a tether that slipped over the side and connected to the neck of a swimming Glagaas. Around him the ship slumbered, even Branson abandoning his post next to the cargo.

The grey bird swam in lazy circles, and occasionally Kaleb would reach into a bag at his hip and throw a piece of Greylin's Glagaas kill into the water close to the live bird.

Minutes drew too hours, the bag was empty and the Glagaas was floating with its bill tucked behind a wing as the Blood Moon held court in the absence of the Ghost who fled in the pre-dawn hour.

Kaleb's eyes drooped and he tapped a slow rhythm on his knee as he sat on the deck, the beat a cadence from a march he'd learned in Academy.

Halfway through a tenth song his hand jumped and he sprang up, eyes searching the surface of the lake. Ripples moved out from where the

Glagaas once slept and the tether line hung loosely against the side of the Tyger.

"Come on…" he whispered impatiently.

Slowly, a black shape appeared on the surface, long-headed like that of a cayman with yellow eyes that caught the subtle light. It slipped through the water toward the Tyger, finally coming to the side beneath Kaleb as two short arms drew out of the black water and claws flashed under the moon.

Kaleb stepped back, the sound of pinched wood drifting up until the long head appeared over the rail. He could smell the ocean at low tide, the stink of it causing his nose to twitch as reptilian eyes studied him.

The creature, near the size of a man, slid over the rail and rested on two bent rear legs, short arms held out for balance as a thick tail flopped down behind.

"Samaya." the thing hissed.

"Candon," Kaleb replied.

The creature tilted its head back and forth, eyes blinking until it raised a clawed finger at him.

"You make tribute?" it asked slowly.

His last word was long and drawn out, a hiss at the end making it sound like there were multiples gifts to be had.

Kaleb nodded, "I do."

The creature crouched low, its tail slithering back and forth.

"What does the Samaya wish?"

"I need to get to the headwaters of this delta," Kaleb said.

"Samaya go to headwater often, cross land…"

Kaleb shook his head, interrupting, "I need the ship to get there."

"Ship too big… too many fords and sand." It said.

"My ship is different, it can cross the land for short distances."

The creature looked up and down the deck, a hiss escaping his lips, "Samaya always like to do strange things."

"Nonetheless, with your guidance, my ship will make the headwater."

"You have more tribute?" it asked.

"Yes, when we reach the headwater."

The creature bowed its head and then went back to the rail. It turned back, hissed over its shoulder, "Three tribute, the headwater, we make a bargain in the old way Samaya, but only for your father and the debt owed."

Kaleb nodded and the thing slipped over the rail with a wet hiss.

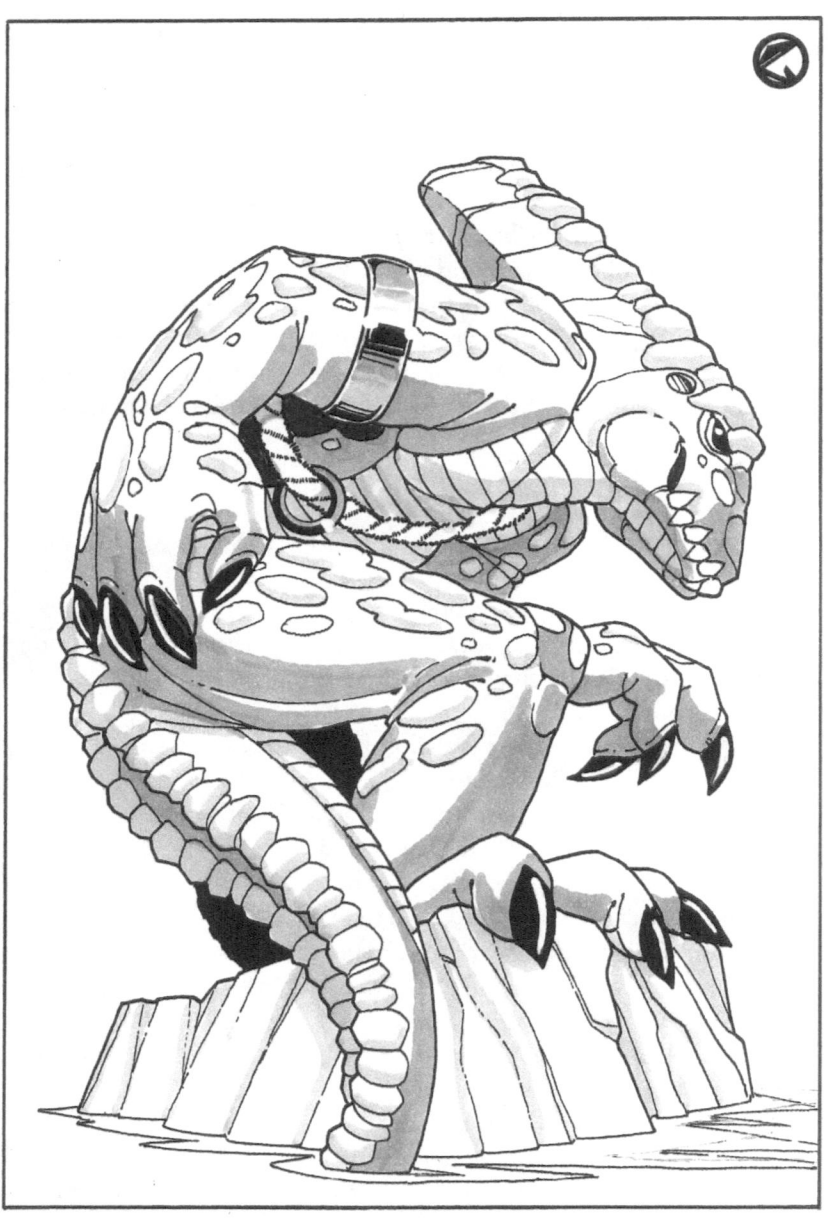

# CHAPTER FIVE

## *SKYLLA*

*I do the captain's service, I find the path, and I play the hand dealt to me by the Saints. There is a free soul inside these bonds, my Enlightened blood swimming in my veins with the depth of the ocean from which it was born, but I serve as duty binds me, be it of my own will or not.*

*Some say I am a whore, some whisper I am a fool, certainly I've been both, but none know the truth save me and my deity. I feel some judgment in you, whatever you may be, but there is no dark ire in you, just a curiosity I think, or so I'll tell myself.*

*My journey continues, and I must be off to duty, but if you watch close you may begin to understand the way of this world and the role of a slave in it…*

The Tyger's motion reversed, the ship lurching slightly as it backed along the channel with half the crew pushing poles against the sandbar to the port.

"Find twelve feet and then engage the lifts Pascal," Kaleb called into the tube.

Skylla stood beside the captain's chair, the weather-eye showing the crew at work and the thinning river beyond.

"That's going to be tight," she said.

Kaleb nodded, "Yes, but if we stay to the port and keep the lift going I think we'll be able to slide across."

The Tyger lurched again, this time the weather-eye's perspective shifting as the horizon lifted up before settling back on an even plane.

"Fifteen feet," Pascal's voice called from the tube.

Skylla took a step toward the wheel but Kaleb caught her wrist. She looked back and he shook his head, saying, "Mr. Gates, keep her to the port, but I don't want her brush-burned on those trees."

"Aye aye, Captain," Morgan replied.

Skylla fell back next to the chair, her lips pressed tight. Kaleb spoke into the engine tube, "Engage the wheels."

Another shudder and the ship hummed for a few minutes before locks sounded and Pascal called from the tube, "Wheels set."

"Give me 3 REM."

The ship crept forward, a third shudder shaking the crew as the ship made landfall and started a slow climb. Below, just on the edge of the sandbar, a black shape slithered across the shallows and slipped into the far side of the ford.

"I don't trust it," Skylla said.

Kaleb turned to her, "That's not your call."

A smell like a coming storm filled the command node and Skylla drew herself away from the Captain toward the starboard stair.

"I'm going down to supervise the crew and see to the cargo if you don't need me here," she said.

No reply followed her as she slipped down the passage, her boots clanking on the metal runners. She entered the starboard deckhouse as Mya opened one of her heavy curtains, the Gola's eyes shaded with azure and touched with smoky grey along her long lashes.

"Have we gone to land again?" Mya asked.

Skylla tried to slip past her, but the Gola blocked her path.

"I can feel his strain even from down here... it's affecting the crew and the safety of the ship," Mya whispered.

Skylla stared at her, the smell of salty brine strong in the air, "What does that have to do with me?"

"You're the cause."

"Me? You're the one not doing her job," Skylla spat.

"My job is impossible when he's too conflicted about what to do with you."

"This has nothing to do with me other than you are looking for a scape-goat."

Mya shook her head, "You have to end this. Either tell the captain you are available, or get him to come to me."

"Available." Skylla paused before raising her voice. "Available! I'm a slave, just as you. To us there is no available, simply what is. Let him take me or no, but it is not a burden or a choice of mine."

Pushing past the Gola, Skylla slipped onto the deck, pressed her back into the shadows of the deckhouse wall, and wiped the tears from her cheeks.

*Why… why does he turn me away when I've offered him everything?*

She ran her hands over her bracers, the metal cool to the touch and the sting of them prickling her flesh as her elemental spark welled in her chest.

The ship jumped and she grabbed rail.

"What was that?" she called.

Branson, near the cargo, called back, "Rock, but we cleared it!"

She wiped the final tears from her cheeks and raced to the rope bridge that connected the two pontoons near the bow nacelles, fingers burning against the thick hemp as she went. Reaching the port deck, she dropped down and moved to the cargo, her hands trailing over the wooden crates until she stopped on one in the middle.

"Is that crate hot or is it just me?" Branson asked.

Closing her eyes, she focused her mind, her spark fluttering and the bands on her wrists and neck burning her skin with a thousand hot pricks.

"Hey, it's leaking!" Branson exclaimed.

Pain blazing through her soul, she released her hold on the box, her boots sliding in the water that poured from the lower corners of the crate. She wobbled, and Branson caught her with one hand, his rifle held aside with the other.

"You okay?" he asked.

There was no water left in her mouth, but she nodded, righted herself and walked stiffly toward the starboard deck house as Parish called the mark and the crew cheered. The Tyger was slowly sliding back toward navigable water.

Five days passed among the tributaries, marshes, and shallow lakes of the delta, the Tyger creeping along at a painfully slow pace until the crew was ragged and the captain a box of dry powder ready to blow at the tiniest spark.

Skylla sat with Arvilla on the bridge, the two having pulled up chairs at the navigator's table as they shared a bottle of Findalynn Vine and threw cards. The weather-eye showed the Ghost Moon, the river sliding slowly beneath as the Tyger sat in anchor and the ship's crew slumbered.

"Morgan is getting better and better," Arvilla said.

Skylla nodded, "The kid's got talent."

"But not as much as you," Arvilla conceded.

Throwing a card, this one painted with a strangled knight, Skylla took a drink from the bottle and looked at the helm. "I can't do every job on the ship… so someone has to replace me at my old posts."

"But still, you've done everything on board, and that's impressive," Arvilla said.

Skylla let her eyes trail to the captain's chair, "All but one."

Arvilla threw a chain-bound gryphon on the knight, saying, "You want the captain's seat?"

"No, and that's a dangerous question."

"Maybe, but you're the one looking at it."

A naked sprite covered the gryphon and Arvilla shook her head and adjusted the cards in her hand.

"How long have we been doing this?" Skylla asked.

"Two years, give or take."

"In that time have you ever seen the captain so…" Skylla trailed off.

"High strung?"

"Yes."

"No."

A fire-maned fox covered the sprite and Skylla took another drink before she threw a two-headed ogre.

"I'm worried," Skylla said.

"The captain's never led us astray before."

Skylla nodded, "That's not what I'm saying, it's just that Mya…"

Arvilla put her cards on the table, slammed a drink down her throat, and then pointed the empty glass at Skylla.

"You forget that witch, especially if she's been pouring poison in your ear," she interrupted.

"But the captain…"

Arvilla shook her head, "The captain nothing! Yeah, I'm sure he has 'needs', but it's a Gola's job to woo a captain and his crew or otherwise they'll put her to port and let the locals have at her. If she can't win him, and mark my words sister, she can't, then she's going to try another angle until all the hells blow up, but that's her problem."

Skylla didn't reply, and Arvilla filled her glass, continuing, "Listen, I've met my fair share of men, and never, ever, have I met one as filled with faith as the captain. It's why the crew stays, because there is something about him that's better than other men in power. He believes in something – honor I'd guess – and that's a hard commodity to come by in the Gun Kingdoms."

Nodding, Skylla took a drink and looked back at the chair.

*Saints save me! I'll either be the doom of myself, this ship, or the man who saved me...*

# CHAPTER SIX

## *KALEB*

*My crew feels it, the tension, the pressure of this crossing, and yet none of them question and none speak out. That is loyalty, something I've worked hard to foster in the five years as captain of the Tyger, and on journeys like this, every former action is magnified.*

*Yet you still watch me, and I wonder what your thoughts on the subject are or if you truly have an opinion at all. I venerate Saint Siegfried the Brave, patron of justice, honor, and chivalry. Are you his avatar? It's a question that plagues me at times because I know you're here.*

*Siegfried is old, three ages separating him from the days when he walked this planet, rode a mighty stead and fought against creatures now only known in fables. Today, his faith is nearly lost, but there are those who still find his works worthwhile, and although we may be few, our purpose is true to a cause that is larger than anything common men can understand.*

*I'll keep to that course, just as I do this river, and if my heart and purpose are pure then the rains will come and the crossing will become something of legend to all the freebooters of the Dragmarsh Shores...*

Kaleb stood on the deck, Skylla beside him and the Candon watching from the rail. The Blood Moon hung low and false dawn was upon the western horizon, as the creature's breath hissed between sharp teeth and its thick tail slid back and forth over the wood.

"You've come to the headwaters, the river is here, coming out of streams and lesser courses dribbling down from the Orthac Range," the Candon said.

Kaleb nodded, "And you've fulfilled the bargain, tribute is yours."

Skylla opened a crate and pulled forth a bag. The sack shook and gobbled as she handed it over to the Candon. The thing reached out, and for a moment his first mate and the creature froze, their eyes staring at each other until it withdrew the bag and slipped over the rail.

Before it fell into the water below it hissed, "Stay well, Samaya, and remember the paths I've shown you."

Skylla fell back a step and Kaleb touched her shoulder. She jerked away, her emerald eyes aglow in the moonlight.

"Skylla?" he asked.

She blinked, pupils contracting as she took a shuddering breath.

"Are you ok?"

Nodding, she backed down the deck, one hand twining around the fingers the Candon had touched.

He watched her go, sighed, and then moved to the deckhouse.

*That was stupid... never let one water-born touch another...*

Ugarth, Tormay, Parish, Greylin and Murwell played a game of cards, the room filled with smoke and the smell of alcohol heavy in the air.

"It's almost dawn, and duty will be early," Kaleb said sternly.

The players murmured replies but kept their eyes on the cards, all save Ugarth who leaned back in his chair and winked.

Kaleb walked past the man and up the stair to the bridge, Yogo hanging against the helm, his eyes glazed and head sagging.

"No lagging, Mr. Stroke," Kaleb said using the boy's newly minted surname.

Yogo popped up, eyes blinking and hands flexing on the wheel. "Yes, Sir!"

Kaleb grabbed a set of binoculars from the navigator's table and headed up the second flight of steps to the aft nacelle.

Wind blew his hair and he tasted rain on the breeze. Raising the binoculars to his eyes, he spied a thunderhead in the distance, great gray clouds set against the growing light of day. From far off thunder rumbled and he smiled.

*Bring the rains. We're going to need them...*

Rain came down in white sheets, the Tyger creating a wake of dirty foam as it cut through the rocky current of the headwaters. Kaleb watched the ship's progress from the weather-eye, his fingers strumming the armrest of his chair.

"How much further do you figure?" he asked.

"Another twenty miles, no more," Arvilla answered.

"Exit points?"

"Three, Sir, the first coming in about five miles: the abandoned silver mine at Kal'abrath," she said.

"Skylla, how about the rain?" he asked.

"Steady, Captain, and I'd say we have at least three more days unless there is a significant shift in the winds."

He looked back at Arvilla, "Time to destination?"

"At 5 REM, without a significant stoppage, we could make Sal'wind Shore in three days..."

"Then Kal'abrath it is," he said.

The Tyger moved on, rain peppering the ship creating a cacophony of sound on the bridge. From the starboard stair Mya appeared, her veil drawn close to her face and a steaming porcelain cup in her hands.

"Captain, I've brought you tea," she said.

She moved quietly across the wooden planks, her eyes focused on Kaleb even as the massive screen of the weather-eye dominated one side of the chamber with images of the storm and the murky shore.

"Thoughtful of you, Gola," he said, taking the cup and tasting it. "Tristran?"

"Dravarian Green," she answered.

Nodding, he went back to watching the screen and Mya bowed and departed the bridge as quietly as she had come.

He continued to sip as the riverbank slowly revealed looming shadows in the gloom.

"We got here fast." Kaleb said.

"Everything is an approximation," Arvilla said.

Nodding, he placed the cup on the arm of his chair and leaned forward. After a moment, he asked, "What do you make of that?"

The rain concealed much, and visibility wasn't more than a few dozen feet, but a wall was visible along the shore.

"A warehouse?" Morgan said.

"No... too low-slung, and there isn't any stonework so it can be a military bunker." Arvilla said.

Kaleb, eyes getting thin, leaned back and shouted in his Engineer's conical, "All stop!"

The Tyger shuddered, and Morgan was thrown against the helm. Kaleb leaned into his ship's communication tube, yelling, "Battle stations!"

His words were echoed all over the ship, the weather-eye catching movement from the structure as something huge rose out of it, camouflage netting falling away and rain washing down from it in a thousand splashing falls.

Impacts sounded on the bridge, the clatter of bullets tacking wood causing Morgan to duck.

"Ease her back, Mr. Gates, give the gunners time to fire," Kaleb said.

The ship shook again, the eight-pounder on the port tearing a chunk from the shoulder of the newly-revealed Tolard Juggernaut as it waded into the river. The metal behemoth's twin mounted machine guns, one on each arm, spat rounds. Someone firing a rifle from the starboard pontoon fell limply back onto the deck.

"Steady..." Kaleb said.

The starboard eight-pounder fired, the juggernaut's hip exploding in a shower of sparks. Men cheered from the deck, but the Tolard adjusted its stance and continued firing.

Kaleb shook his head, "Pascal, engage the lifts."

The Tyger rose above the waves but the Tolard swiveled and matched the rise with a ten-pounder tracking the course in its chest.

"Brace yourselves!" Kaleb yelled.

The ten-pounder fired, the port nacelle exploded and the ship tilting sideways. Morgan clung to the helm and Arvilla was thrown off her feet.

"Pascal, give me 10 REM!" Kaleb shouted into the conical.

"She's listing to port, the helm won't control that kind of a surge!" Pascal's voice was distant and full of carefully restrained frustration.

Kaleb looked up, the screen hazy with water pouring down the now unshielded weather-eye.

"Pascal, I need thirty feet... give me enough push for thirty feet!"

He stood, slid a step, and then pushed himself forward to the helm. Morgan let go and Kaleb pulled the wheel around, the Tyger groaning with each inch as it adjusted course to aim straight at the behemoth.

The Tolard loomed as a shadow in the darkness of the downpour. As the storm drenched the attacker, a swirling in the air like a waterspout rose up around it. A heavy gust of wind shifted the Tyger to port once more, Kaleb falling away from the helm and Pascal calling warnings over the conical.

Water poured over the weather-eye but the view still provided a shaky image of the Tolard, its machine-guns tilting up and firing impotently into the sky as a swirling gale swept over it. Another shot rang out from the Tyger's starboard nacelle, the round striking the Tolard in the chest, the wind swirling so heavy with water that the machine lost its form on the screen and became a dark blur.

Pascal's voice kept on coming out of the conical, the Tyger lifting again to a level plane as the weather-eye cleared. Ahead, the Tolard fell, a twister of water and wind ripping metal plates from it as it plunged backward into the river.

A wave swept out from the fall, the Tyger lifting and falling with it, part of the port nacelle dipping dangerously.

"Take the helm, Mr. Gates!" Kaleb yelled.

Gates got to his feet and dashed to the helm as Kaleb stumbled to the captain's chair, his right hand turning the conical toward him as he stared at the weather-eye.

"Pascal, bring us to full stop and keep the lifts engaged."

"She's taking on water, Captain, and I'm not sure how long the lift will hold."

Kaleb looked at the turbulent waves, parts of the Tolard still exposed above the surface. The thing remained still, rain beating down on it in unabated showers.

"Captain..." Morgan pointed toward the screen.

Kaleb looked away from the Tolard, his eyes following those of Morgan until he saw a small figure on the shore. The downpour helped hide it among the Tolard's old cover-hedge, but it still created the outline of a man in a trench and hat.

"Pascal, what about the wheels?" Kaleb asked into the conical.

"The port isn't going to engage anytime soon... this place is a mess."

Kaleb nodded, his eyes still on the figure, "*Who are you?*"

Arvilla descended the steps from the aft nacelle, water dripping from her bare skin and a pistol still in her left hand.

"Report," Kaleb said.

"The Tolard is down, and a man stands on the shore. Stoneham wants to take the shot. What are your orders, Captain??"

Kaleb stared at the figure a moment longer, then leaned into the conical, "Stand down and prepare for emergency grounding."

Morgan turned back to Kaleb, saying, "Captain?"

"Just keep her steady, Mr. Gates, and try to maneuver the port nacelle over the Tolard as I'm going to use it as a dry dock," Kaleb said.

Morgan nodded, and Kaleb spoke into the engineering conical, "Pascal, keep power to the lifts and give me 1 REM."

"Aye aye."

"Arvilla, get to the nacelle and send Stoneham down the steps so he can relay, we're going to need to know when to stop."

Arvilla disappeared up the steps and the sound of heavy boots followed soon after as Stoneham appeared in the frame.

"That guy was waving his hands as the Tolard took a dive, Captain, and I'm figuring he's…" Stoneham trailed off

"Enlightened… yeah, I got that feeling as well. Still, let's deal with one disaster at a time."

Stoneham nodded and the Tyger slipped slowly across the water, Morgan fighting the helm to keep her straight. It took three minutes of Stoneham calling out positions from Arvilla until Kaleb signaled a full stop, water pouring in from the nacelle's open hatch and Stoneham full-on drenched from the shower from above.

"Disengage lifts," Kaleb said.

The weather-eye dropped, the port rising slightly and the sound of groaning wood echoing through the ship. On the shore, the figure was gone, and as the Tyger came to rest Kaleb leaned back in his chair and sighed.

"Good work, Mr. Gates, you've earned your pay today."

Morgan sagged against the helm, smiling wanly at the compliment as the sound of driving rain hammered the ship and waves lapped around the injured, beached craft.

# CHAPTER SEVEN

## *SKYLLA*

*Yes, I felt it, the elemental surge. What of it? These are the Wastes, the place beyond the fringe we normally trade, and strange things are out in these parts. The Candon was only an example, his water-born nature like a breath of fresh air to my suffocating soul, and yet it was nothing compared to what I felt in the attack.*

*These bands around my wrists drive fire into my blood, they wrest my very nature from me, but still I can smell, I can taste, and I know what is waiting out there for me if I only wish to take it.*

*My captain plays a dangerous game, one so much deeper than any cargo or epic delivery, but it's his place to make such decisions and learn from his mistakes. Whatever the case, I'll continue on as best I can, but now that I have a taste of the forbidden I can only dream about having more…*

The crew stood on the shore, hats held at their chests as rain continued to punish them. Kaleb stood opposite the long line of dark figures, two muddy graves lying between. The Captain's voice cut through the shower, the words sinking into them all.

"Murwell and Gage were good friends, good shipmates, and men we were all proud to call brothers-in-arms. They will not be forgotten, just as all those who have gone before and will come after won't be forgotten as long as the ship remains.

"We give thanks to their service and their sacrifice, and we return them to the earth that they may be reborn from it..."

Skylla stood, her head downcast, but she shifted nervously from foot to foot as the eulogy went on.

*I feel you... out there, just beyond the thickets... what are you... Human? Jai-Ruk? Aspara?*

Kaleb finished his speech, Stoneham and Tormay saying a few additional words of parting before the procession broke up, most going back to the two small launches pulled up against the lapping waves along the shore.

"You have the look of the lost," Kaleb said.

Skylla looked up, her hand pulling away from where is caressed one of her bracers.

"What?"

"The lost, you look like you've lost more than most on this ship," he said.

"Oh... well, it was a tough go."

Kaleb stared at her a moment and then adjusted the collar of his trench, eyes moving to the east and the thickets looming on the horizon.

"This weather isn't going to help us with repairs, and the word from Pascal is that we might be completely crippled without a few new Dalan Power Cells."

"Well, we're pretty far from a smugglers port, so I hope that's not true," she replied.

They stood, silence stretching out between them as the boats pulled away from shore. When the first launch got to the Tyger, Kaleb turned and sighed, "You want to meet our mysterious savior?"

Her cheeks flushed pale blue at her jaw and a smile stirred on her lips before sliding away to nothing.

"Captain?" she asked.

"I know you sense the Enlightened, hell, I can practically feel him on the wind, so don't play coy with me. We haven't the time."

She nodded.

"Now," he began. "We've got some ground rules, and the first of them is no touching, understood?"

Another nod.

"The Candon was one thing... but a full Enlightened is another. Whoever this person is, they had a reason for doing what they did and I'm certain it wasn't to help us, so keep that in mind."

"Yes, Captain."

He studied her, eyes dark beneath the brim of his grey hat.

"Right, then let's go for a walk and see what we might scare up among the brush."

The Tyger had long ago vanished from her view, the woods and rock outcrops having concealed it a half-hour before when Skylla finally pulled up. Kaleb stopped behind her, a hand in his trench and his eyes on the woods.

"You're a long way from home, Samaya," a voice called.

It held a lyrical quality, like wind whistling through pipes, but it was certainly male, rich and pure.

"And you're a long way from the grave the politicians and priests tell us you've all gone to," Kaleb replied.

There was a laugh, a lean figure moving from behind a tree. It was a man, tall and slender, with a head of long wavy black hair and skin the shade of milk-touched chocolate. He wore a gunman's duster, broad-brimmed hat, and in the dark he could have been mistaken for someone from Kaleb's military unit.

"Very true, but still, that doesn't change the fact that you're far away from your home territories," the man said.

"We're traders, and sometimes that means finding less-traveled routes," Kaleb said.

The stranger stepped closer and a foreign wind picked up, the rain drops scattering around him without actually touching his clothing. He studied their equipment with a knowing eye.

"Well-armed traders at least, but you're no wiser than most…"

Kaleb's hand twitched, and Skylla took a step forward to change the subject, "We wanted to thank you for your help."

The man looked at her, his eyes so blue they made the sky seem pale by comparison.

"And who are you?" he asked.

"She's Skylla, my First Mate, and I'm Kaleb Cross… and to whom do we have the pleasure of our proffered thanks?"

    "My name is Ethran Tha, and it's a pleasure to make your acquaintance Miss Skylla," the stranger replied, directing his answer to the water-born.

    The wind brushed her cheek, the rain breaking around her as the Enlightened lifted a finger and waved it before him. She sucked hard at the air, the smell sweet and intoxicating.

    "Mr. Tha," Kaleb said.

The Enlightened didn't look away from Skylla, his eyes pulling her in. "Ethran, please," he said.

Kaleb's revolver slipped its holster and the wind died, rain splattering Skylla's cheeks as the Ethran's smile faded and the world grew cold.

"I need to know why you helped us with the Tolard," Kaleb said.

Ethran, turned, his left thumb playing against the middle finger of his hand. "I'm no ally with Samayan automatons, especially relics that lurk in deadzones waiting for easy prey."

"So it was coincidence that you arrived just as it attacked?" Kaleb asked.

"I didn't say that. No, I'd been watching your progress for two days as I've never seen a ship that size make it this far into the headwater."

Kaleb slid the pistol back into the holster and Skylla let out a breath. At the same time, Ethran let his hand fall to his side.

"Well, it looks like we both did each other a favor. So we can call it even," Kaleb said.

"But the ship?" Skylla said.

Ethran raised an eyebrow, "Is there something wrong with your ship?"

Kaleb turned a dark eye to Skylla, but she didn't back down, instead looking at Ethran and saying, "We need new Dalan Power Cells if we're going to continue."

"Skylla!"

Kaleb's voice was harsh, but Ethran held up a hand, "Fear not, friend, your first officer has done you a service because I know the whereabouts of many an ancient Samayan artifact."

"Really?" Skylla said.

Ethran smiled again and the bands at her wrists and neck burned until she rubbed at them.

"I already feel like we've overstepped here, Mr. Tha, so you'll excuse me if I don't inquire further," Kaleb said.

Shaking his head, Ethran held up his hands, "Please, I've nothing to gain by watching you die on the river or having to travel cross land into the wilds. If you don't accept my help, you're throwing your life away, which I won't try to dissuade you from, but think of your crew, Captain. How many more graves will have to be dug on the shore before you take a hand offered in kindness?"

Skylla turned back to Kaleb and he wiped rain from his chin with the back of his hand, the downpour increasing in volume.

"How far is it to these cells?" he asked.

"A week, perhaps more if the rains have flooded certain passes," Ethran answered.

Kaleb shook his head, but Skylla stepped in, saying, "Captain, what choice do we have?"

"Little, unfortunately, but a two week turnaround might cost us the trip anyway..."

"But it won't cost us our lives or the ship," she said.

Kaleb sighed and then offered Ethran his hand. The Enlightened looked at him a long moment and then took it. They shook.

"We'll be here in on the morrow, at sun-up, and I'll take you at your word that we really are friends," Kaleb said.

Ethran smiled, "Absolutely, Captain, I'd have it no other way."

"It's a dangerous business, Skylla," Arvilla said.

The two were packing, their shared room very close quarters as they stuffed backpacks with gear.

"He's Enlightened, like me, I don't think we have anything to worry about."

Arvilla stopped and turned to Skylla, "You do remember that we Samaya rebelled against Enlightened bondage, and have hunted your species to near extinction for more than a century?"

"That was a long time ago..." Skylla said.

"Genocide is genocide, and people tend not to forget that fact."

Skylla shook her head, "You don't understand."

Arvilla caught her arm and swung her around. One of Skylla's hands went reflexively to the daggers at her thigh.

The elder woman's brown eyes held steel as she said, "Listen, you stay clear of this strange Enlightened, for your own good and that of the crew... they can't be trusted, he can't."

"They?" Skylla hissed.

Arvilla didn't back down, and the smell of the sea slithered into the room as the bracers and choker sent shocks through Skylla's bones.

"Yes, *they*, because *they* aren't a member of this crew," Arvilla answered.

Skylla showed her teeth, then grabbed her pack and walked out, Parish getting knocked over in the process as he came down the hall.

The storm still raged outside, the river having risen enough that the ship was level, anchors having been thrown to keep it in place. Pascal was hanging from a rope on the port pontoon, a firebrand in hand and a mask over his head. Sparks flew and hot metal hissed as the sheets of rain flung themselves relentlessly against the ship.

Skylla marched up the deck from the nacelle and slipped into the starboard deckhouse where she dropped her pack, her hair soaked from the brief journey bow to stern.

"Skylla?" Mya called.

She bit her lip, a curse nearly escaping. The hangings on one side of the chamber were pulled back and Mya, veil in place, looked out.

"I thought I smelled the sea. What has you upset?" Mya asked.

"Leave it be, Mya."

Mya came out of her lair, hands raised in mock surrender. "I'm the ship's Gola, and I'm here to help you through your troubles as best I can."

"I said leave it be!"

Mya took another step and Skylla lashed out, her hand coming up to strike Mya in the chest. The blow sent the taller woman back and she lost her balance, falling hard to the floor.

"Skylla!" Kaleb yelled.

Skylla froze, Kaleb standing at the bottom of the stair to the bridge, his face dark. She stepped back to the opening of the deck but he yelled again, "Stand down!"

She held her ground, Kaleb coming into the deckhouse and helping Mya to her feet. The Gola clung to him, painted eyes narrow as she stumbled once as she seemed to struggle for breath.

*Bitch... you knew he was coming down...*

"Are you alright, Gola?" he asked.

"I'm fine, I must have slipped on the water from Skylla's opening of the deck door." Kaleb stared at her a moment, both her hands twined around his arm.

"It's my fault, Captain," Skylla said.

He turned to her, "Damn right, and this isn't done, but for now I'll have you at the launch. See it prepared because I don't want to be late."

Skylla nodded and then backed out, the rain a comforting blanket to her soul as she moved across the rope bridge to the port pontoon where Stoneham loaded supplies into the smaller boat.

*This isn't over... you've got that right...*

# CHAPTER EIGHT

## *KALEB*

*Can she be trusted? If she can't then the entire basis of my belief system has been wrong for more years than I care to count. And yes, I knew exactly the risks I was taking with her when I started this journey, although I didn't think Enlightened exposure would be this great a lure.*

*The Apsara, a wind-born, is another matter entirely. He's working an angle, make no mistake, and I fear it's going to get deadly before this whole things shakes out in the end. Still, all I can do now is stay the course, step with caution, and keep my faith that those I've trained and brought into my world are strong enough to withstand any temptation...*

Kaleb stood at the shore, rain still coming down and his away team standing in a circle. At the ship, Tormay, Pascal, Gates, Olaf, Branson and Mya stood along the port cargo rail and watched, with Gates waving a goodbye.

"Doc, I'm going to say this one more time, you don't have to come," Kaleb said.

Rose shook his head, water spilling off a dipped reservoir in the top of his velvet hat. "You're going to need me more than Pascal will, and besides I'll do more damage on board than I will out here. I'm a doctor not a mechanic."

Kaleb nodded and looked at those around him. The youths Greylin, Parish, and Yogo carried heavy loads on their backs, each armed with a rifle. Stoneham also carried a rifle, this one with a modified binocular site, as well as a short blade weighted at the head for taking down brush. Bosun Lancaster and Mid-Tech Tolbert both wore pistols and carried long spears, and Arvilla hefted a small revolver and walked with a bayonet also hung from her belt.

Skylla had her nail gun and twin throwing knives. Her backpack was slung low into the small of her back and her rain slicker covering her from her neck to her boots.

"That's it then," Kaleb said. "Keep your eyes open and your weapons ready because for all I know we're walking into a trap."

The crew nodded, all save Skylla who kept her eyes on the distant thickets. They began walking, boots sucking into the mud as they made their way into the trees. The sun was kept at bay by the clouds, a semi-dark of grey settling under the newly budded bows.

Rocks like the heads of old giants rose up among the woods, their faces green with moss. It was old country, the feel of ages seeping into the company's boots along with the water.

"How many years since Samaya lived here?" Tolbert asked.

"Half a century or more. I'm not really sure," Kaleb answered.

Tolbert was from Taux, his skin tan and his hair shiny black and kept long. He wore tech coveralls, and had a half-dozen talismans around his neck, most resembling keys.

Doc Rose spoke up, "I'd say more like a full century if I remember right, this territory was abandoned after General Malett used Torg Gas to clear the Enlightened uprising in the Skii'Mount province."

"Torg Gas is outlawed," Parish said.

"By the Tristran Accords, yes, but those laws weren't in place during the War of Steel and Bone," Rose said.

The party drew closer together, and Tolbert asked, "Is it true Torg can lay dormant for years if undisturbed?"

Rose nodded, "Yes, especially in low lying protected areas or even in the ground."

Thunder boomed above as if to drive the point home, and a ripple of lightning backlit the trees like dark hands reaching up from the earth.

Thirty minutes into the journey bones, bleached by years of sun and polished by the current rains, poked up from the ground as the party slid down a defile amid torrents of running rainwater. Crumbled stonework lay scattered about, yellow grass having grown up through it as vines slithered over the surface. A bell, three feet high and two inches thick lay on its side in their path, rust covering the surface and the interior hammer missing.

Kaleb kept the crew going, eyes warily watching the surrounding wood until they entered a clearing on the far side of the abandoned settlement.

"We wait here," Kaleb said.

The party shook packs off shoulders and found shelter where they could, the rain insidious and unrelenting.

"Did we have to come during the rainy season?" Lancaster asked.

"Stow it, Caster," Skylla said.

Arvilla, leaning on a tree next to Kaleb, asked, "How much farther?"

"This is the place where we found him, so we'll stay here until he shows up."

The navigator looked around, "If we could get into the heights, get a vantage, we might not need him. I'm pretty sure I can read the habitation signs and lead us to this 'lost city.'"

"After a hundred years and in this rain, I doubt it," Ethran called from the trees.

Rifles went to shoulders, but Kaleb raised his hand, "It's the guide."

Ethran appeared, his hat pulled low and a pack slung over his back.

"You're late," he said.

Kaleb nodded, "The morning muster took longer than anticipated, but we've still the full afternoon and evening ahead."

"Skylla," Ethran bowed, seeming uninterested in Kaleb's explanation.

Skylla nodded, and Kaleb frowned, "Again, this isn't a social call, Mr. Tha, and as you've made it abundantly clear we're already late."

Ethran smiled at Kaleb and then turned his back on the party, saying, "It's a long journey, and this rain will hinder our course, so keep close and stay upon the path I put you."

Stoneham slipped close to the Captain, "I don't trust this guy."

"That makes two of us, but we need those cells or we lose our ship," Kaleb whispered in the same tone.

Stoneham checked the bolt on his rifle, and Arvilla flanked Kaleb on the opposite side with her hand resting on her pistol. Kaleb watched Skylla muster the rest of the men, and then move up the path until she was not five feet from Ethran's back.

*It will be a long journey and I don't have the patience to babysit a moon-struck girl.*

The camp was dry, the outcropping of rock in the lower elevations a perfect break from the incessant drizzle and a fire a blessing to pruned and cold fingers and toes. Five days had passed under the stormy skies, and the party had marched to a bone-weary pace up the slopes of the Kii'Torin Hills until their only companions were the wind, the cold, scrub grass, and stone.

Ethran kept to himself, the Enlightened hovering at the edge of the camp as usual, his back to the party and the fire. Skylla reclined close to Kaleb, her eyes staring across the camp at their guide as the fire popped and cracked.

"What do you see in him?" Kaleb asked.

Skylla turned, her face crimson in the firelight. "You wouldn't understand."

"Try me."

She let out a long sigh. "It's not that I see anything in him, but it's impossible not to feel something… like a magnet drawing me close."

"He's dangerous," Kaleb said.

"You're dangerous," she replied. Leaning up, she got within two feet of his face, "Besides, why would you care about any of my feelings anyway?"

Averting his eyes, he looked at the fire, "You're a member of my crew, my first officer, and you're my responsibility."

"Is that all?"

He kept looking straight ahead. "Yes."

She turned back over, saying, "Actually, I'm your slave."

"Those are unkind words," he said.

"It's an unkind world, and as far as you're concerned and I wear these bonds, I'll need to remember that."

She was silent, and he watched her back rise and fall, the angle of her head still pointing toward Ethran.

He opened his mouth but Stoneham passed wind in his sleep and Greylin and Parish started waving their hands about and laughing.

Skylla rose up and hissed at the two young men, "Stow it!"

They settled down, as did she, and Kaleb took out his journal, the leather tether holding a protective flap closed. He slipped the knot loose and pulled out a pen. The writing cylinder held two tiny runes that ensured ink was ever present on its tip… a gift received on his graduation from the Academy from his father.

Opening the journal he wrote a few words concerning the day's travel, then flipped back a couple of pages and sketched more detail to a map he'd drawn there. Mountains jutted up around the dotted path they'd travelled, dangerous waterfalls, and a dozen ruins were on the pages as forests clung to life among the some of the climbs.

Pausing, he turned to Skylla, her back still to him, and then flipped forward to where he'd stopped writing. The pen set a moment on the yellowed page before he started sketching, Skylla's back coming into view in the image, then the fire, and finally a dark shadow beyond her horizontal shape… *Ethran.*

Beneath the picture he wrote, *the days are long, and the nights longer still.*

Tethering the journal, he replaced it in his coat and then fell back into his bedroll, the roof of the cave like a dark blanket above.

The wind was scathing, coats and scarves whipping like loosed sails as the party crested another rise, the grey face of a mountain to their left and a thousand-foot drop to churning whitewater on their right.

Their path was once a road, now crumbling, cracked, and long-forgotten, that crept up the heights in constant switchbacks that teetered on the edge of oblivion once every hundred feet.

Ahead, Ethran called a halt and moved back toward them, the company pressing their backs against the rock-face and catching their breath.

"There's been a collapse ahead," Ethran said once he was close to Kaleb.

"You mean worse than we've already faced?" Stoneham asked.

"What's your call?" Kaleb asked.

Ethran looked down the slope at the party, then back to Kaleb. "It's going to be tricky, but we could attach a guide rope and everyone should be able to make it."

Kaleb nodded, yelling, "Yogo, bring up the rope!"

The youth crept up, his pocked face red and wind-burned and his eyes wild as he kept furtively looking at the precipice a few feet away.

"Easy, kid, it's not as bad as it looks," Stoneham said.

Yogo nodded, pulled off his pack and grabbed a length of circled hemp rope from within. Stoneham accepted the coil and removed a hammer and some iron spikes from his own pack.

"Show me the way," he said to Ethran.

The two ventured further up the road and disappeared around a bend, the sound of a hammer's strike sliding through the air as the party waited.

"What fool would build a city up this high?" Arvilla asked.

"Air captains," Doc Rose said.

"Air Ships? Flying in one of those is as crazy as building cities on mountain tops," Arvilla replied.

"True, but if this place housed that kind of firepower and tech, then the odds of finding the cells we need are pretty good," Kaleb observed.

Stoneham came around the bend and waved, the company sliding up the wall until they saw the slide. It was a like a titan's maw, jagged teeth of stone coming up to sing hissing songs in the wind, the cliff face having given way as a new thin waterfall tumbled down into its ever-empty gullet.

A thin lip of stone persisted against the fall, the edge no larger than the span of a middle finger. The rope had been pinioned across the span three feet above the lip, half a dozen spikes hammered into the exposed face.

"Keep your eyes on the line, go slow, and stay close to the face," Ethran said.

The Enlightened scout was on the far side, his hair a mass of blowing curls and his eyes lit like blue fire.

Stoneham pointed to the far side, "I'll stay here, captain, and see the lads across. You take the first run."

Kaleb nodded and started across, his boots sliding along the edge as tiny bits of stone tumbled away into the void below.

It took no more than a minute, but it felt like much longer, his breath heavy in his throat and his hands numb against the rope he held tight. When Kaleb completed the journey, Ethran helped him to the side and waved Skylla across.

She took the rope, her long violet hair swirling in the gusts that seemed to increase around her with each step. At the half-way point she turned to look back to the company and Stoneham waved her on. She turned her focus back to the face, took another step, and a sudden, gale-force wind swept down the stone above and tore her feet right off the edge.

For a precarious moment she hung against the rope, but the wind, like a vengeful beast, turned back and pulled her away, fingers slipping from the line as she tumbled out into open air.

Kaleb screamed, and Skylla echoed his call, but she was gone, falling deathly fast toward the churning water and slate-grey rocks below.

Poised at Kaleb's side, Ethran took two steps and plunged into the air after her, his coat whipping around him and his arms outstretched. The party leapt up to the edge, all eyes watching as Ethran increased his speed and caught hold of Skylla half-way down, the two tumbling together until they splashed into the river below and were gone to the clinging mists.

Kaleb clutched the edge of the road, his eyes casting freezing tears across his face as the relentless wind howled in its victory around him.

Stoneham was calling something, and Kaleb finally slid back against the wall as he wiped his eyes with the back of his gloved hands.

*She's gone... and I was never brave enough to speak my mind.*

# CHAPTER NINE

## *SKYLLA*

*I feel the air... my stomach churning as the mountain slips past. This is my death, my last sight as I slip beyond the binding threads of this world and enter the next.*

*Do you know me now? Do you know the torment in my soul that I came so close to my freedom, to a final truth, only to be denied at the very threshold?*

*Let the darkness descend, let the fell scythe of doom reap me like a blade of withered wheat... I care not... it is done and I must be prepared for my final judgment.*

Skylla sat up, a scream slipping from her lips and echoing in the thundering vault around her. A wall of water tall and wide as a galleon mast poured down behind her resting place, the light of day showing through the streaming falls and mist.

She was naked save for her bracers and choker, her clothes hung over a boulder close by as a sheltered fire warmed the cotton pallet where she'd slept.

"Hello?" she called.

Her words bounced around the cavern and were then swallowed up by the falls. Gingerly, she moved, but her body held no pain and she slid from the blankets, pulling her clothes from the rock. Dressing, she stood and looked around, the cavern slipping into deep shadow behind and two drying packs nestled next to the stone.

She leaned down and touched the second pack.

"Ethran..." she whispered.

A swirling tendril of air caressed her fingers and the fire guttered. She rose, eyes searching the gloom until she saw a figure approaching.

"I see you've finally woken," Ethran said.

"What happened?" she asked.

"Well, you fell... or don't you remember?"

She narrowed her eyes, thoughts playing in her mind... *the climb, the switchbacks, the rope...*

Sucking in a breath, she drew her hand to her mouth and leaned back against the boulder.

"I thought..." she said.

"Well, if you hadn't been with me, yes, you would have died."

He was close, the sweet smell of him tickling her nose and the bracers tingling at her writs. She looked up, Ethran smiling, his face charming and flawless in the muted light of the cave.

"How?" she asked.

"I'm Aspara, a wind-born, and my skills lend toward bending the air, harnessing it, and channeling the flow to help make me who I am."

"Can you fly?"

He shook his head, "No, not exactly... the best I can muster is this..."

Wind swirled, his coat flapping as he raised his arms, the tiny tornado of air lifting him up from the stone a couple of feet before his settled back again.

"Incredible..." she whispered.

"Enlightened hold their element dear, it's why we are who and what we are."

He came close, knelt, and poked the fire with a stick.

"Indeed, and it's what you are as well." he said cautiously.

She rubbed the bands at her wrists.

"I never truly understood," she said.

He looked back at her, an eyebrow raised. "There is a great deal I can teach you if you let me."

She didn't speak, and he stood, his hand reaching out to take hers. Her hand pulled back and he stopped, watching her with his cobalt eyes until she nodded and reached for him.

The touch was like a shuddering release, his element calling to her, digging through her defenses and splashing against her soul like an enveloping and warm wave. She gasped, legs giving out and she fell into him, his arms holding her close as she struggled to breathe.

Tears slipped from her eyes, the bracers and choker prickling her, but his element stayed them, forced back their magic and kept her warm, safe, and at peace.

"Freedom... it's all the Enlightened have left, and yet they've done their worst and taken even that from you," he whispered.

Sobs caught in her throat, and he pulled her tighter, stroked her hair and whispered sweet words as the thunder of the falls sheathed them from the world.

Ethran tramped the last of the fire out with his boot, black smoke rising as grey ash puffed up with each impact.

"Where do we go from here?" Skylla asked.

"The real question is, where do *you* go from here?" he questioned in reply.

She sat a moment on the boulder, a piece of dried and salted meat between her fingers.

*Where indeed... and why?*

"Your friends, they'll have made one of two choices: either retrace their steps two days and try to find a passable trail to follow the river looking for your body, or they will have gone ahead in search of their precious cells."

*Kaleb will go forward, his duty to the crew far greater than whatever feelings he had for me, and that's assuming there were any to begin with.*

"This vault," Ethran began with a wave. "It is connected to the old Samayan mines, their kind having dug out a honeycomb beneath this range searching for ferrous metals, or so they'd have the world believe.

"Instead, they were using Kin, making them find the purest veins before smelting the ore in their godless forges for the purpose of war."

She looked around, the vault was virgin and without a strike of pick or hammer.

"If you wish to seek your friends, I can guide you through the caverns to the long stair, and from there we can take the journey up to the city in hopes of finding them before they leave. I warn you, however, I'll not be of much use to you in here, the earth is my opposition element, and being beneath it draws out my wind-born strength quickly."

*Kaleb, my master, do I abandon you like you've surely abandoned me? This is my chance to escape, and yet I hesitate because I know the code you follow and I've tried my whole life to follow it as well.*

"You'd do that for me?" she asked.

He looked back at her and smiled, her heart jumping in her chest.

"Indeed, I've already leapt from a thousand foot precipice for you, what are a few hours in a cave compared to that?"

She nodded, "Then I request your help, Ethran, to find my Captain and my crew."

He paused a moment, his eyes staring into her before he nodded, the Enlightened grabbing his pack and offering her a hand. She took it, the two of them wandering back into the darkness of the cave as he pulled a black-tipped rod from his pack.

The fire-stick glowed to a distance of twenty feet, its shine creating no smoke, but the heat from it made her face dry and she stayed back a few feet as Ethran worked the trail. Their time inside the caves had drawn out until she wasn't sure how much had passed, but Ethran's breathing had become labored and sweat trickled from his brow.

"Should we stop?" she asked.

He shook his head, whispered something that was lost in the dryness of his throat and continued on.

They'd long since left the natural vaults, the pick and hammer-chiseled mine a warren of twisting passages and dead ends. Up-shafts sometimes loomed in darkness over their heads and a hissing drifted down from shadowy tunnels when Ethran shined his light there for too long.

Once, along the path, the light shone on a patch of gold laced into the rock. Its sparkle was like the dreams of a thousand greedy men were poured into the cracks of the world, but Ethran passed it by, his boots moving ever on.

"I'm sorry," she said.

He didn't pause, his legs shuffling, but his voice carried over his shoulder, "Don't be! What must be done, must be done."

Pulling hands around her upper arms, she nodded, their path cutting up another rise until Ethran stopped short.

"What?" she asked.

He raised a finger to his lips, "Shhhhhh…"

As if in answer a chorus of hisses slithered back from the central mine, the new chamber stretching out before them in four layered, tracked, and tunneled glory.

Ethran raised the wand and then threw it forward into the chamber, the light playing off the walls until is skittered to a halt in the center of the room. Shadows sprung forth. Dark shapes the size of dogs – although lower to the ground and broad as a lady's divan – burst from unseen holes and challenged the light.

Skylla pulled her nail-gun, raised it to her shoulder and waited. Ethran pulled forth a long thin blade from his trench.

The beasts hissed, wings shaking and buzzing as though communicating some message like bees in a garden. The largest of them came forward with amber pinchers open and long antenna waving at the fire-stick.

"Steady…" Ethran whispered. "They've been tracking us and they think they've won."

The creature, now looking little more than an enormous roach, touched the stick, the glowing tip flaring in white-hot brilliance as Ethran yelled, "Now!"

He leapt forward, his sword lancing the head from the nearest creature. Skylla fired a nail into the largest of the cluster, the long silver dart piercing the thing's head and pinning it to the stone floor. Both wounded creatures kept moving, the headless one spurting green fluid and running about while the pinned one scratched the floor with six wild legs.

Ethran kept moving, his white blade slicing down again but he stumbled, the next roach sidestepped, and he just clipped its wing. Skylla trained another shot on the wounded creature, the nail ripping through its torso and spraying green blood on the far side. It hissed and jumped at Ethran who parried it away, severing a mandible in the process, but two more of the creatures had turned toward him and were fast approaching.

Skylla drew a third shaft from her quiver, loaded the gun, and hit an oncoming roach dead on in the face. The nail ripped a hole from the thing's forehead all the way to its tail and the beast skidded to a stop without so much as a twitch.

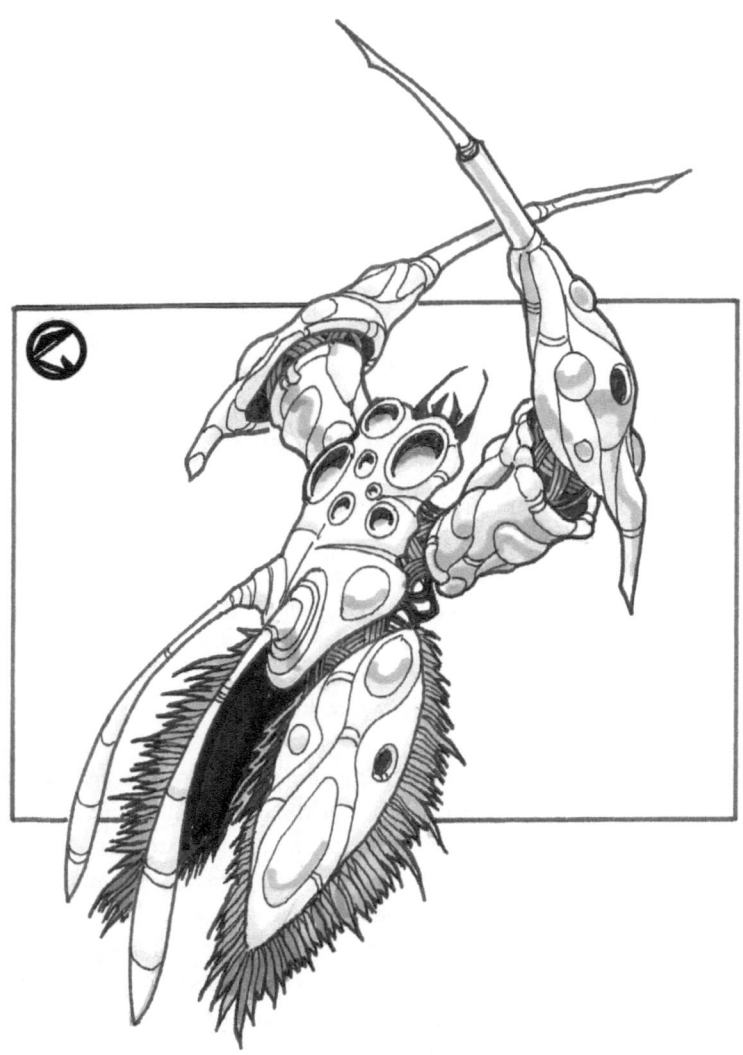

Ethran swung again, this time removing two legs from the second of the newcomers, but the previously wounded roach came again and he had to adjust his stance to kick it away. The maneuver left his flank open, and the missing leg roach slid in and bit him on the right thigh.

He screamed, and Skylla loaded another nail, fired, and pinned a roach that had crept along the upper passage to the wall above Ethran's head.

The wind-born's blade fell again, this time taking the head off the roach that bit him, but its mandibles remained attached, blood trickling down the man's pants.

"Ethran!" Skylla screamed.

He pierced the head of the missing mandible roach and staggered back to her, more of the creatures coming out of the ground near the still flaring stick. Ethran fell into Skylla's arms, sweat pouring down his face and his breathing like that of an aged chimney sweep.

"Hold..." he wheezed. "On."

She took hold of him and he closed his eyes. Wind swept through the tunnels with a great groan, the sound like a dragon coming to life. The roaches hissed and beat their wings, but were momentarily confused.

Around them, a whirlwind appeared, Skylla's hair whipping around her face as Ethran closed his arms around her waist. She did the same around his neck, and the air lifted them both, roaches finally coming to hiss and snap in the area they just vacated.

They ascended with the funnel, rising ten feet and then twenty into the vault until the wind pushed them over a metal track that ran to a series of small shacks and shelters on the third level of the annex.

Skylla's feet touched down and the wind died, Ethran collapsing with it. She held him close as she laid him on the ground. His eyes were closed and his breathing a series of short intakes.

"Ethran?"

He didn't reply. She stood, looked around and saw a metal cage nearby, vertical bars of steel and a heavy cable framing and attached to it.

"Elevator..."

Tucking his blade in her belt, she dragged him across the tracks, boots thumping against each wooden tie.

"Stay with me, Ethran!" she whispered emphatically.

Below, the roach's shrill calls were a chorus of noise, their wings beating like an orchestra. Skylla dared not look over the lip to see what they were doing.

She pulled, strained, and finally made the lift. The metal frame was closed and she laid Ethran down, hands gripping the crisscrossed wire of the door. She lifted and the metal shook but didn't give. She tried again as the hissing below grew in volume, but the door wouldn't budge.

"Saints, please..." she prayed, straining against the metal.

Another pull, this time bits of rust shaking loose. She stepped back and kicked the frame twice with the heel of her boot. Ethran coughed, stopped breathing, and then coughed again with a great wheeze.

She gripped the wire frame again and gave a great heave. The metal groaned but gave, the exterior door opening up two feet before it caught. Skylla let go, grabbed Ethran, and pulled him under the lip until he rested against the wall of the back of the box.

On the track outside, black shapes appeared, and Skylla crawled back to the door and pushed down with all her weight. The door slid closed with a metallic thump, and the roaches' antenna twitched all around as they swarmed in.

Reaching up, she pulled the interior wire door down, this one moving easily into place before she spun around in the gloom looking at the interior walls. Somewhere below, the hissing came to a crescendo and the flare dwindled, the light fading away as dark shapes struck the elevator and clanked against the metal.

Darkness fell, pitch as the grandest midnight, and Skylla could smell the stink of the creatures around her, hear their hissing, feel the metal groan with their attacks. Her fingers slid across the walls, touching, moving, feeling until she finally found a lever that was covered in dust and locked in the downward position.

"Saint Frommer… see this slave… hear her prayer." she whispered.

With a heave, she pulled the lever up. For a moment nothing happened, but then a light flickered to life in the top of the box, the rheumy yellow glow showing dozens of roaches swarming the exterior of the cage beyond the box.

The sound of gears working above started the bugs hissing again, but they could do nothing as the box shuddered and then rose above the throng. Skylla fell to her knees, the box exiting the vault on its course to someplace above.

# CHAPTER TEN

## *KALEB*

*It's the crew that matters, the fate of the ship, not one slave I rescued from the auction block five years ago. In the final reckoning, she should not matter at all.*

*I keep telling myself that, keep hoping the words will make sense to me, but you know the truth don't you? It's wrong, all my feelings, my emotion, but I can't help the dread I know in my heart... the sense of utter loss as visions of her falling keep playing again in my mind.*

*The world is lessoned somehow, but I must go on for the men and women who still depend on me. This is just another loss in a long line of them, and as much as I curse the Saints for taking someone else I care about, there has to be a purpose.*

*Am I right? Only Siegfried can know, or perhaps you, but I feel as though the world is a ship tumbling on the waves of a trackless and troubled sea... all sailors drown there, and it's only a matter of time until it happens.*

Kaleb sat in the tower, his journal in hand and the rain having turned to snow outside. Wind broke like a wave against the heights and sounds like a dying moan slithered through the stonework of the structure in haunted voices.

A fire was stirring amongst the rubble of a crumbled wall, snow turning to a wet mist that darkened the stones where Greylin sat with his rifle and watched the morning light paint the newly frozen mountains a shade of honey-pink.

Kaleb sketched a picture of Greylin where he sat in the opening, the caption read, 'a long watch over the breaking dawn'.

Stoneham snored beside him, Arvilla brewing a pot of coffee from melted snow and grinds she'd nursed along the journey.

"It looks like no rain today," she said.

Kaleb gave a grunt, "Yep, just snow instead."

She removed a tin cup from her pack and poured the steaming coffee into it. Kaleb kept working on a description of the tower they now occupied, the structure fifty feet tall and hanging precariously over a huge divide. The top level contained a pinwheel with rusted gangways, chain tethers still in place for attaching gas ships in high winds.

"Captain?" Arvilla asked.

He looked up and she offered him cup of coffee.

"Thanks," he said.

Wrapping his fingers around the cup, he blew on the surface, wisps of steam rising up with the smell of warm and distant lands.

"You know, I'm no Gola, but you can still talk about it," Arvilla said.

Kaleb took a sip, nodding, "I know."

Arvilla took a drink herself, both of them staring into the fire until she broke the silence once more.

"She talked to me sometimes."

"What?"

She shrugged, "Skylla wasn't a fan of the Gola, so when she was upset or had issues with something she'd talk with me instead."

"I'm not sure that helps me now." he said.

Arvilla took another sip, "Perhaps, but it might give you a measure of closure if you knew how she felt."

"Felt about what?" he asked.

"You."

He turned with shaded eyes, saying, "Arvilla, I'm a Naval officer, and when men die in combat the survivors don't sit around rehashing old memories. It just doesn't work that way."

"You forget, I'm a soldier as well, but in the Hilani we honor out dead by never forgetting them, and stories of those we've lost give us something to fight for."

They stared at each other until he nodded, took a long drink, and then sighed. "You have your ways, I have mine, but tonight it's all too fresh."

She nodded, "Very well, Captain, but if you don't go to see the Gola when we return to the Tyger, you know where to find me."

Closing his journal, he stood and stretched, saying, "Let's make a promise, that both of us will get back to the ship in one piece, and from there we can tell stories."

Arvilla smiled, teeth white against her dark lips, "Agreed!"

The party slogged through a foot of snow, the covering drifted to three feet in some areas as the grey clouds still threatened and the spring winds blew warm but potent gusts among the twists of the high road.

Stoneham broke the trail, his scarf wrapped around his face and an iron pole – appropriated from the tower ruin – checking the footing.

Kaleb trailed the leader, Arvilla as his side and the rest of the company trailing behind in a long line of grey. The morning light cut through the clouds in huge golden pillars beyond the next rise, and a white-tip hawk soared on updrafts above.

They marched on, Stoneham the first to top the rise and he stood there, waiting for the rest, his eyes looking east. Kaleb joined him, the mountaintops beyond like deadened ivory tusks. The closest, however, was grey and lit by a golden column of sunshine.

There, lying in spiraling layers and lofty towers of glass and steel was a city of dreams. Bridges, domes, colossal buildings, boom cranes, and dark spires collected snow and shimmered in the sun.

"Kii'Tora" Stoneham whispered reverently.

"How could they have abandoned this?" Arvilla asked beside him.

Kaleb shook his head, the rest of the company straggling up to stare across the white expanse to the forgotten metropolis.

"I never believed it really existed," Tolbert said.

"There was a time when the world was whole, five centuries of healing having taken place after the end of the Streambenders and the rise of the Enlightened. The world is filled with wonders lost to the Samaya and Enlightened alike, and this is just another tomb built by hands long forgotten," Doc Rose said.

They stood a long while, wind whipping their coats and hats until Kaleb tapped Stoneham on the shoulder and pointed down the road.

A thousand feet further down the bend two huge towers sat, a gate between them and a suspension bridge trailing out behind to the city across
the gorge. Stoneham nodded and pushed forward, his iron staff keeping a
slow but steady pace until the towers loomed close. From a hundred feet,

ancient etching became distinct on the great iron doors. They spoke in languages long–since lost to Samayan scholars.

"What do you make of them?" Kaleb asked.

Stoneham looked up shielding his eyes from the sun above. "They're a fine piece of work, but it looks like someone left them open."

Between the two forty-foot doors a sliver of light trickled through, and snow had collected in the opening.

"Remember," Kaleb began. "We have no idea what might have been left in this place, or if those who fled the Torg Gas placed traps behind to surprise those who might come after."

The party nodded, some mumbles of agreement passed between them. Stoneham marched on, Kaleb close at his heels as they came to the opening, his iron staff beating away the collected snow until it connected with something beneath.

They paused, Stoneham pointing back and the party retreating several steps. He continued to clear the snow, the iron striking something again until a skeletal hand was exposed, then another, and finally a skull.

As the party watched more bones were cleared. It was this grisly barrier that had kept the gate from obtaining a full seal.

"What do you make of it?" Lancaster asked.

"A lucky break," Arvilla said.

"But not so for the victims. These bones are probably left from people fleeing the gas and they died where they struggled to get clear of the city," Doc Rose added.

Silence fell then, and Parish said a prayer to Saint Shera as he pulled his hat from his head. Stoneham continued to clear the bones, and as the party broke through the tangle of remains and the winter drift the bridge beyond was no less eerie as frozen skeletons lay in a veritable graveyard that hung in the sky two thousand feet over the crevasse.

Kaleb picked his way between the bones, Stoneham breaking the trail and the spring wind swirling around them from along the span. On either side the mountain gave way in jagged cliffs of grey stone, views of distant vales and waterfalls decorating the country on either side.

"The Skii'Mount Province must be something in the summer," Arvilla said.

Kaleb nodded, "Now that I'm here, I'm starting to understand why they built on this spot. Not only is it breathtaking but it's incredibly defensible."

"Unless you use gas…" she added.

A hundred yards beyond the first bridge a crevasse opened, and second makeshift bridge of bone spanning the distance.

"Someone has been here after the fall," Stoneham said.

Kaleb nodded, but the party kept moving, the bone bridge creaking precariously as they made it across.

The city looming up ahead, the dark metal of the place turning to a more subdued burnt orange as rust crept along its facade. The far gate was standing open, the bones dwindling among the ironwork and pavestones as the snow wrapped slithering white fingers around structures, but the drifts were nowhere to be found on the streets, having been cleared by the cutting wind.

"I wonder who was the last person to see this place alive?" Parish asked.

"General Malett I'd guess. They say his airship dropped the canisters that doomed the city," Doc Rose answered.

Kaleb called for quiet, every spoken word drifting off into the forgotten ruin with a hollow reverb. The buildings beyond the gate were a mix of stone and metal, glass in the lower levels having shattered into spiderwebs over the now opaque panes.

Aged signs hung on the outside of most buildings, the main gate once housing a merchant's quarter. They picked their way through several build-ings, most goods inside rotted or rusted away. They found an apothecary, barber's shop, tavern, dry goods supply, and a dress shop before Kaleb called the searchers back to the street.

"What do you make of it?" he asked Stoneham.

"Very little sign of movement here, but the snow is fresh and covers any other sign. Still, Captain, I'm not convinced we're alone up here with that new bridge and all."

The youths kept their rifles close at hand, eyes searching the streets that twisted away in all directions.

"Keep close," Kaleb ordered.

They moved on, Stoneham keeping on the main road leading to the heart of the old city which rose up in a huge collection of towers and glass domes. Bone piles were constant reminders of those that lost their lives in the place, some much larger than others as though bodies had been placed together by survivors before the end.

Carriages with horse skeletons still in harness, a child's overturned tri-cycle, and dozens of other relics lay upon their path. The clouds continued to break apart above, and their light revealed more lost memories in open windows and side streets.

They were within sight of the final rise to the city center; the area was a collection of concentric, circled gardens now dry and overrun with tall brown grass. Suddenly a sound echoed through the city. It was metallic and heavy, like a ship sliding against another. The foraging party turned with weapons raised.

Around them silence returned, and Arvilla leaned close and whispered in Kaleb's ear, "Captain, what was that?"

He shook his head, Stoneham calling for them to move once more. Kaleb lagged a bit, his eyes scanning the empty street which they'd travelled.

*I don't have the heart for the truth… because that sound, like a cackle from the grave, was the city closing its mighty gates.*

# CHAPTER ELEVEN

## *SKYLLA*

*I've come out of the darkness. I've risen from the grave and been reborn. You see this, you are my witness and I take full responsibility for what is to come. These bonds around my wrists and neck, they are abominations, as is the Captain I fought so hard to love.*

*In what world are people kept like pets, metal rings around their necks and no say in their very existence?*

*Ethran has opened the world to me, provided a view I didn't know existed and shown me the beauty of my lineage that I was denied by the Samaya who fostered me until the uncaring gavel struck at auction. Now, inside this forgotten and dead city I have risen like the fabled phoenix, and I will flower and bloom like the coming spring as long as Ethran is at my side.*

*Together, we'll see this world reworked and the injustices brought against out people made right. Kaleb will be made to understand, and if he doesn't then so be it, but I'll not return to the life I once thought such a gift.*

*Today is my first day of freedom, and I will relish it like only a once shackled soul can.*

The antennae of the roach still twitched and felt the air as Skylla pried the mandibles open. Ethran grunted, a bit of wood clenched between his teeth. Blood spurted out of the wound, and Skylla cast the fractured head away to the back of the elevator box and inspected the damage.

"It's not too deep," she said.

Ethran nodded, and Skylla drew out alcohol and dressings from her pack as she started to work on the wound. He leaned back, head against the wall, the chamber around them cold and barren, but open windows stared out into the sky and his breathing and color were much improved.

She worked slowly, carefully, and the bandage wrapped the leg tightly before she was done. Ethran reached out to touch her hair. She froze, his fingers rubbing the violet locks between thumb and forefinger as he stared at her.

"Violet hair is an oddity... even among Enlightened," he said.

Looking away, she started repacking her bag as her heart pounded in her chest and the bands at her wrists burned.

"I know, it's a terrible color," she said.

He laughed, "Not from where I'm sitting."

She turned back and their eyes met, a long moment shared before she forced a breath from her lips and then smiled.

"I'm not sure how well those creatures can climb, but I'd say its best we get moving," she said and then looked down to his leg. "Assuming you can walk."

He nodded, "I'm tougher than I seem."

"So I've seen." she whispered.

Ethran stood, hand pressed against a wall as he tested his leg. There was a noticeable limp as he took several steps, but he shook his head and motioned to her.

"The sword," he said.

Reaching into her belt she withdrew the weapon. It weighed almost nothing, the blade a milky-tan like aged ivory with runes carved into its entire length. The hilt was a cross-piece of coral, polished smooth and blue as the sky with a grip wrapped in soft leather and topped with a flawless sapphire set in the pommel.

"It's a strange weapon," she observed.

He took it, turned it over in his hand and brought it horizontal before his eyes, "I've carried it a long time. It's become a friend."

"Magic?" she asked.

He laughed, "I'm Enlightened, what do you think?"

"Sorry, but it doesn't even look like metal."

"That's because it isn't. Aspara don't take well to things of the earth: stone, iron, and such. Those trappings do not appeal to our wind-born nature. Still, we've ever been in need of weapons, and our smiths found ways to create implements of war from other things, like bone."

She stared at the blade, asking, "Does the magic keep it from shattering?"

"Indeed, and it keeps it sharp as a barber's razor, but the real measure of its worth is in its original form."

"I don't understand."

"It is dragon bone, as is any good Aspara blade worth its master."

"Dragons are a…" Skylla trailed off.

"A myth? Maybe in Samaya culture, but they once roamed this world just as did Streambenders, Saints, and even Gods."

"How can you know that?" she asked.

He smiled, "Because I've known several dragons."

"But…"

Turning away from her, he sheathed the blade and started from the room, calling over his shoulder, "You've much to learn, Skylla. This world isn't really what they want you to believe."

He disappeared, and his slave companion stood a moment before grabbing her pack and running to catch up.

Three levels, all connected by natural bridges, lay behind them. The lower city was a place of open sky views, shabby cells, and grey stone. Skylla walked beside the enigmatic wind-born. His stride had eased as he continued to move, and she kept pace with her nail-gun in her arms.

"These were the Kin quarters. You can tell by the scrollwork on the walls," he said.

In most of the cells, the walls were covered in pictographs, the stone swirling and mixing in a labyrinthine-like mosaic of images.

"They must have been great carvers," she said.

He laughed, "I'm sure they'd be offended to hear you say so."

"I don't understand," she said.

He stopped, rubbed his leg and then took out a wooden canteen. After taking a drink he recapped the lid and answered her implied question,

"Kin are high earth, the diametric opposite of Aspara. They aren't carvers, they're shapers. Everything you see here done by sheer force of wills that were pressed against the stone to form those images."

She looked around, the artwork sublime and beautiful in the shadowed light provided by the scattered windows.

"High earth. But if that's true, then why all the windows?" she asked.

"Good question," he said, and then he reached out to tap the canteen against one of her bracers.

She looked at them and then back at the openings, saying, "The Samaya wanted to keep them off balance?"

"Indeed, and although those bands you wear are effective, they were costly and in the days of the War a population this big couldn't be shackled with the kingly trinkets of the Samayan Tome Mages."

"Then why didn't they just rise up, drive the Samaya out?" she asked.

He sighed, "There is a reason this place is dead. The Torg Gas wasn't for the Samaya above, it was for the Kin and other Enlightened rebels below."

"Saints preserve" Skylla whispered.

"I don't think they much care, but I guess it never hurts to ask," Ethran replied.

Returning their canteens to their packs, they moved on, their steps echoing in the tunnels as they continued to rise.

Morning gave way to afternoon, the wind from the climbs warm, and nesting birds playing among the clefts as grey stone gave way to rusted metal. They paused in an exposed garden court, the air sweet with the smell of spring and the sun bringing heat to the unkempt greenery still clinging to life. Skylla leaned against the court's rail, the earth stretching out forever below her.

"I think I can see the Tyger from here," she said.

Ethran, sitting on an old bench, took out some jerky and said, "That's not such a long shot. If you had a spyglass, you just might be able to pick out the headwaters springing up in the far west."

Skylla turned, her hair blowing in the gusts and a smile on her face.

"What's so funny?" he asked.

"This life, I guess. One moment we're being chased by carnivorous bugs and the next we're viewing breathtaking vistas from the top of the world."

He nodded, "It can be like that, especially in the deadzones."

"How long have you been out here?"

"That's hard to say," he answered.

She frowned and he shrugged his shoulders, "Life is complicated, Skylla, and it's hard for me to explain immortality."

Pushing away from the stone lip of the garden rail she moved over and sat beside him. They took some food, sharing his canteen, and finally she looked back at the horizon and said, "When you said you knew dragons did you really mean it?"

"Yes."

"How old are you?"

He sighed, "I've lost count, but at least three millennia have passed since I first took my steps on this world."

She shook her head, eyes turning to him with tears around the edges. "How can that be?"

"Apara are of the immortal wind. It is our gift."

"And what of me?"

He smiled, "I cannot say. Your true nature is unreadable to me because of the bonds you wear." Ethran glanced meaningfully at her wrists.

Skylla touched the bracers, a shadow falling over her. Looking up she saw a dark shape, thirty-five feet from head to tail sailing between her and the sun. Beyond the creature, half a dozen more blue and white shapes slipped across the sky, huge tails swirling the wind as they plied the trades across the ariel range.

"Sky Whales." she whispered in wonder.

Ethran stood, a hand going to his mouth in a kind of cup. He made a call, the wind rushing up around him. The closest of the mighty floating beasts turned back with dark eyes to stare down at him.

He raised a hand and the behemoth heaved closer, until the wind-born was able to stroke the smooth skin of its nose. It made a call, a deep throated moan that sent the grass around the garden bending back, and Ethran laughed before turning back to her.

"He wants to know who my friend is," he translated.

"What?"

"He's not met you before, and he wants to know your name."

She shook her head, "How can you?"

"They have limited telepathy, but he can't connect with you because of the bracers."

She took a tentative step forward and the beast opened its great jaws, hundreds of sharp teeth white against its pink tongue.

"Come on, this isn't something that happens every day," he said.

He offered her his hand and she took it, stepping up until the smell of the thing, like wind and heavy rain, bled into her pores and made her tremble.

"Go on" the Enlightened encouraged her.

She reached up, her fingers sliding along the whale's flesh. It was damp and smooth, a layer of water making her fingers hydroplane across the surface.

The whale moaned again and Skylla was covered in a warm mist as she stepped back into Ethran's chest. He held her a moment and whispered, "He thinks Skylla is a pretty name, and he likes your hair."

She smiled and the beast showed its teeth once more before swishing its great tale and slipping back into the open sky. It whirled in the wind once then swept away, as it followed the course of its fellows toward the northern horizon.

"I never knew they were real." Skylla said softly.

"We – the Enlightened – kept them inside the Shining Cities until the Streambenders were gone. Otherwise they would be just another fable told around Samayan fires. It was our goal to retain all the life we could, and in many ways we were greatly successful," he said.

"I've been so blind all this time," she whispered.

Ethran held her in reply, his arms wrapped firmly around her waist. Skylla laid her head back into the small of his neck, wondering what other revelations awaited her.

"There are a million things to learn, and I'll teach you everything. But first we've got to find your crew. Only then can you be free of the bonds the bind you, and I know if you speak your heart, Kaleb will hear you."

She closed her eyes. *I pray you're right, and I pray I can face him with those words ready to fall from my lips.*

# CHAPTER TWELVE

## *KALEB*

*I feel as though the streets cry out with the silent screams of a thousand ghosts, this place a grim reminder of what my kind has been capable of in the not-so-distant past. I've known these things, I've read of such battles in the history books of the Academy, but those accounts are written by the victors.*

*One can only imagine what was done here, what horror was perpetrated on all these people, both Samaya and Enlightened alike. Whispers among the elders of the admiralty staff told stories different from those in the books, bits and pieces taken from the lips of old air-sailors who saw these atrocities first hand.*

*Now that I walk among the ruins, I know what is true, and that truth cannot be found in books. This is a cause not worth fighting for, and a part of me wishes that my colors didn't still sit upon my shoulders in this naval coat.*

*Still, I stand on the threshold of something better, and I'll continue to pursue the just path, the righteous path, and never will I judge a person on their birth or the blood that runs in their veins. All I can do is look them in the eye and pray that I glean some true meaning there.*

The first set of stairs were made of iron, full sections rusted away, with the scrolling metalwork coming apart to the stone foundations below. They passed it with some difficulty, Kaleb always keeping an eye on their rear, but nothing came from the streets as the sun continued to slip across the sky.

The next set of risers were white marble, the unchanging stone having fared much better in the elements, and their path moved up between two mighty towers. The stone and steel monoliths held metal doors, but no windows until thirty feet above the ground level, and these were made of broken glass.

Beyond them a dome stood, the roof half collapsed and wind howling among the exposed metal supports. A set of green, patina-tinged double doors stood at the top of the stairs, a pattern of gryphons etched into the copper surface.

"A gryphon wing... that's the sign of the Air Armada," Tolbert observed.

Kaleb stepped up next to Stoneham, the two of them standing two flights of stairs below the door.

"Did you hear the city gate?" Stoneham whispered.

"Yep."

"Then we've limited time."

"I know," Kaleb said.

Kaleb turned to the crew, noting their weary faces in the golden light of the late afternoon.

"This is an Air Armada building, from the size it is probably a hanger, so keep your eyes peeled for those cells," he said.

The crew nodded, Arvilla removing her pistol from its holster and Doc Rose cleaning his glasses with his handkerchief.

Moving up the final two flights, Stoneham checked the door with his staff, the iron ringing against the copper like a gong.

They waited, Stoneham turning with a smile, "Looks like no one's home."

No one laughed and he turned back and pressed his shoulder into the door. There was a groan, the hinges sending a screeching echo through the city. The hairs on Kaleb's neck stood on end, but he didn't move, and the city remained dead and silent behind him.

The doors gave way, but Stoneham only opened them enough for the party to slip through in single file, the inside as large as any storage depot in the mercantile district of Findalynn. Full sections of the glass roof had collapsed, but in some spots the now opaque glass and iron still held, snow having dribbled through the openings and clinging precariously to existence in the cool shadows of the interior.

"Stay frosty." Stoneham reminded them.

Kaleb drew his pistol and pulled back the hammer as the thuds of the company's boots drifted through the hollow shell.

"Parish, Greylin, you two take the south. Yogo, you're with Stoneham and the Doc to the north. Lancaster and Tolbert take the west side and Arvilla and I will sweep the east," Kaleb ordered.

The party broke up, the mostly two man teams picking their way among the rubble. The floor was covered with a series of rails like a train annex, and chains thick enough to hold a small ocean vessel hung in clusters from similar rails that laced a box frame just beneath the great curve of the dome overhead.

"I didn't realize the damned things were so big," Arvilla whispered.

He followed her eyes to the north, Yogo and Stoneham moving slowly beneath the suspended superstructure of a half-complete gas ship.

"The frame is aluminum, so it's lighter than it looks, but yeah, they're pretty huge and the cells they used to power them were legendary," Kaleb said.

"Still, I can't imagine one floating over the land, or being inside its belly."

Kaleb nodded, "They say that after the war Malett hid his flagship, the Sky Drake, before the Reclamation Council could ground and destroy it like the rest of the armada, so I guess there's still a chance for you."

"I'll stick with the Tyger, water twenty feet beneath you is a lot more palatable than the ground at five thousand."

They kept moving, the east side of the bay a collection of fabrication facilities with nothing of value within. Kaleb checked several prefabricated cabins that sat against the east wall, the framed rooms like boxes of a children's puzzle that could fit together in several different ways.

Beyond the stand-alone rooms, another door stood, this one locked, with the Academy symbol for priority storage hazy on the front panel.

"What do you make of this?" he asked.

Arvilla knelt down before the door, eyed the keyhole and then pulled her pack off her back.

"I don't know, but give me five minutes and we'll soon find out."

He nodded, turning to check the dome as a whole. Only Parish and Greylin were in sight, the two climbing over an old rail car that still sat on the tracks. It was covered with metal rungs. Pulling out his canteen, Kaleb took a swig and looked at the sky above. What was left of the roof softened the late afternoon sun, but the area fully exposed to the sun's rays showed signs of deep wear, the elements slowly eroding their viability.

"It's a sad world when places like this cease to exist," he said.

Behind him the click of metal sounded and he turned. Arvilla put away her picks, and he stowed his canteen.

"After you," she said.

He stepped to the door, grabbed the handle and twisted. There was a grinding of metal and then a buzz. Behind them a klaxon sounded for less than five seconds before its blare faded to a strangled end. Several lights flashed red in the vault above.

"I'm not liking that" Kaleb muttered to himself.

The staccato sound of gunfire erupted at the west side of the dome, a shape lumbering from the snowy shadows as it cast blazing rounds at the rail car. Parish and Greylin both leapt behind the car, bits of debris flying over their heads as the assault went into full bloom.

"Damn!" Kaleb swore.

He slid sideways and found cover beneath a workman's table, Arvilla at his side.

"What is it?" she asked.

"Another automaton, something third generation and probably unkillable."

From the north a rifle sounded, a heavy caliber round ricocheting off the walker's shielded neck and turning its attention. It swiveled its cone-like head, two concave half-spheres spinning and whirring as it trained its machine-gun toward the old ship frame.

Bullets spewed forth again, steam rising from the weapon's cylindrical canister and smoke snaking out of the barrel.

Two more shots came from the west, these impacting on the thing's side plates as they sent sparks showering out with each impact.

Again the thing whirred and turned, the gun blazing above its right shoulder, while on the left arm a blade snapped into place. The monstrous machine moved several more steps, adjusted its stance and showered the darkness of the western dome with blazing green tracer rounds used mainly by the Air Armada.

Light from above fell upon the automaton in its new position, and Kaleb could see the heavy armored plates, the thickness of the body. It looked for all the world like a massive, armored knight. It was a nine-foot-tall masterpiece of a forgotten age, the stink of newly tilled earth permeating the area around it, a by-product of the earth magic that drove its lifeless body.

Parish and Greylin had found their guts, both lads rising from behind the rail car to fire into the thing's flank, causing it to turn again. This time its gun remained silent, gears whirring as it marched toward their position, its shining five foot blade at the ready.

"Saints asses!" Kaleb cursed.

He stood, pistol pointing at the thing's head and fired a shot. The bullet pinged off the plate, but shrapnel from the lead round tore through one of the 'eyes'. It was a lucky shot, and the automaton stopped moving when his ocular sphere stopped spinning.

The other orbit spun wildly, the thing turned and Kaleb jumped behind the table just before bullets rained down on the position.

"That was both brave and stupid, Captain," Arvilla said dryly.

Kaleb pulled his hat low, the sound of the thing's gigantic feet pounding the floor reverberating off the wall behind them as it approached.

Kaleb looked at the wall. The door was slightly ajar.

"You ready to run?" he asked.

The navigator nodded, and together they leapt from behind the desk and sprinted toward the door. Bullets trailed them, debris exploding in all directions as they burst through the open portal, closing it quickly behind them.

The tick and tack of rounds pinged against the metal, and Kaleb fell back breathing hard. Beside the door, Arvilla leaned against the wall, her hand at her side as she gave him a wan smile.

"Ouch," she whispered.

Blood dribbled between her dark fingers, a stain growing in the dense fabric of her coat.

"Keep low," he said and she nodded.

More rounds struck the door and he looked around the room. The place was filled with a metal desk, several dusty and dry open cabinets, and a large metal locker at the back. He ran around the desk, the locker as tall as he was and closed with a large lock at the handles.

Behind him three feet of a blade penetrated the door, causing Arvilla to gasp.

"Come on…" Kaleb hissed.

He raised his pistol and fired at the lock. It spun but held, the enemy's blade withdrawing and then coming through the door again at a lower angle.

Drawing back the pistol's hammer, he fired a second round, this one shattering the lock. Behind, the outer door shuddered from a fisted impact, and Kaleb pulled the broken lock free and threw open the inner doors. Rifles stood in an upright row at eye level, five pistols beneath and on lower shelves boxes of cartridges were stacked. He leaned down, pulling paper boxes free that disintegrated in his hands, bullets spilling out on the floor around his feet.

"No... no... no!" he whispered, each box coming apart upon inspection, until a wooden case at the bottom held firm beneath the press of his fingers.

The door shuddered, the hinges groaning as the blade twisted in the metal and tore a hole the size of a man's head in the center of it.

Kaleb grabbed the box, flipped the brass catch, and pulled it open. Inside, eight rounds lay in a velvet mold, two long and four short. They were forged of honey-oricalcum, every inch of them covered in detailed scrollwork.

He pulled one of the smaller rounds, thumbed the cylinder release on his pistol and loaded the bullet inside an empty chamber.

The door gave, Kaleb turning as he snapped the cylinder closed and raised his weapon. The automaton's head slid into view, the machine-gun leveling off just as Kaleb fired.

Metal against metal rang out, and then there was nothing, the automaton holding steady and quiet as though it was a statue.

Kaleb let loose a long breath and lowered the pistol, a groan coming from Arvilla where she lay next to the open door.

He rushed to her side, propped her up, and her eyes opened.

"Captain..." she mumbled.

"The doc's coming, just hang on."

She smiled, her teeth pearly white and he bit his lip as an ache crept into his gut.

"Captain" she said again.

His hands shook, but he forced himself to nod. Her eyes stared past him, through him, and she kept smiling like she had the first day he'd seen her in Ebontra. It was her way.

With a final shudder she went limp and he leaned back, and his hand reflexively went out to close her eyes. No tears came. He was numb, his mouth dry and his stomach churning bile into his throat.

Stoneham was the first to the door, the man sliding under the automaton's blade and coming to a halt when he saw Arvilla. Yogo and Doc Rose entered next, the doctor coming over and kneeling beside Arvilla before he sighed and shook his head.

"Damnable monstrosities" Doc whispered.

Stoneham looked at the frozen machine, "I don't smell the earth anymore."

Kaleb shook his head, stood and marched back to the locker. The open box lay on the floor, bullets still in place. He leaned down and pulled the three remaining pistol rounds and slipped them into his trench pocket, then grabbed the final two rifle cartridges.

Stoneham walked close, his hand going out to touch Kaleb's shoulder.

"She'll be missed," he said.

Kaleb nodded and then placed the two bullets in Stoneham hand, saying, "You know when to use these."

Stoneham looked down, slowly nodding as Kaleb turned back to the front of the room.

"Doc, I'm going to need you to get her ready for transport. Yogo, she'll be your responsibility, understood."

The young man nodded, as did the doctor. Moving past them, Kaleb slipped under the automaton, past the questioning faces of the rest of his waiting crew, and marched toward the tower of sunlight streaming through the open roof.

There, he raised his hands, closed his eyes, and took a long breath, the sun warming his skin.

*Find your ancestors, Arvilla… and I promise I'll speak of you often.*

# CHAPTER THIRTEEN

## SKYLLA

*How can someone judge me who hasn't walked in my shoes? I can feel your dislike of my actions, but what do you know of such things?*

*Have you carried the weight of a collar around your neck? Have you sat amidst a leering crowd as they checked your teeth, admired your naked form? Were beatings a full course of your childhood?*

*These were my lessons, the challenges placed before me, but I never gave in to them and I never gave up. There is a reason I'm the first officer of the Tyger, and that's because I worked for it every second of every day for three solid years.*

*What I do now I've earned as well. The Samaya kept me in ignorance, but now my eyes are open. Judge me or don't, but you'll not change my mind in this lifetime…*

Skylla walked beside Ethran, their path twisting up the side of the plateau as the city hung around them on shafts of iron driven deep within the stone. The estates of the wealthy hung like birdhouses along the cliffs with aerial gardens, empty fountains, suspension pools, and viewing solariums reflecting light as the bright day turned to the amber glow of late afternoon.

Ahead, an empty waterfall and viewing bridge spanned between two rose-quartz towers. Ethran stopped in their shadow as he looked up at the levels above.

"Another hour, maybe two of sunlight, but we'll not make it to the upper city before dark with so many broken paths and forced turn-backs on our course," he observed.

Skylla nodded, her boots clanking against the metal frame of the bridge before she stopped on the arched apex of the span, hands gripping the rail.

Looking up at the naked cliff above, she asked, "What happened to the waterfall?"

"Without magic to keep it flowing, it died like the rest of this place."

She looked down, a sense of vertigo twisting her stomach as the world lay several thousand feet below.

"It must have been beautiful..." she said softly.

"It was."

She turned to him, smiling, "How incredible is it to have seen so much?"

"'Incredible.' Yes, I suppose you could use that word, but it's sad as well. Remember, everything I've ever seen is gone now, save a few small relics here and there."

They stared at each other a moment, the wind playing tricks with both their long hair. Finally, Ethran's expression changed. He chuckled, saying, "I've got something I want to show you."

He led her over the bridge, more spiral stairs twisting ever up until they came to a large half-circle court. The ring stretched around a cathedral with twin spires, thirty foot stained-glass windows, and a gold-studded set of double doors.

"What is it?" she asked.

"The Sky Church of Saint Shera," he said grandly.

The building was made of white marble, veins of deep burgundy running through it, and not a single piece was hand-carved. The entire structure looked like it had been cut from a single block of stone.

"It's beautiful," she said.

The wind-born took her hand and led her up the steps, the doors swinging open with the slightest touch of his hand.

"Saint Shera is a patron to many things: brides, mothers, family; but above all else she stands for hearth, home, and a place to rest your head."

Inside, the building was warm, a tranquil glow coming from the windows above the doors. She turned, stared up at the panes that recreated the image of a woman with long chocolate hair turned to gold at the tips. Her face was long and lovely, skin tan and eyes as blue as the summer sea.

Around her were images of tankards, children, glowing fires, and a procession of women dressed in colorful gowns.

"Did you know she's married to Saint Erik, patron of thieves, gamblers, and philanderers?" he asked.

She shook her head, amused, "No."

"They say that in the Fifth Age, when the old gods were cast from the world, she fell in love with Erik. At that time he was a simple Human mercenary, and she an Aspara innkeeper. For her, he gave up the throne of the old Empire, and for him she accepted the burden of being the wife of a wandering soul. Both were elevated to sainthood for their romantic sacrifice."

He paused a moment, then added, "For the world, Saint Erik had a thousand faces, but for her, he had just one."

They walked further into the main hall, and as she gazed up into the light, the figures in the glass came alive in her imagination.

"Shera... hear my call," Ethran intoned solemnly. "We are travelers and have come for your service."

Skylla turned at his words, and was surprised to see that upon the flagstones in the middle of the hall a rug had suddenly appeared, complete with pillows, blankets, and several bowls of fruit and tankards of beer. Ethran stood next to the collection smiling as he raised a hand and waved her forward.

"How?" she whispered.

"The priests of the Samaya are mouthpieces, and their faith is based on guile and an overwhelming desire to quell their people. They've long since turned from true faith to a business arrangement in which they fleece their followers with promises they themselves don't even believe.

"Here, however, is a true church of Shera of the old Orders, and I am a true believer. Shera's kindness still rests in this place. For those like me, her blessings ring true and I can have sanctuary in one of her halls, just as in the old days."

Skylla sat down on the rug, savoring the thick fabric as she stretched out her legs and let her fingers swim across the surface.

Ethran took up a tankard, drew in a hearty mouthful, and swallowed, a smile washing over his face as he gave a great sigh, saying, "There's nothing like the blessings of Shera. I envy Erik his damnable luck for winning her heart."

Skylla picked up a tender fruit, the skin pale pink and the flesh soft as she bit into it. Juice ran down her chin and she raised a hand to catch it, more fluid squirting from the sides of her mouth. It tasked like milk and honey, and she laughed as she drew it from her lips, juice dripping on fingers, chin, and the rug beneath.

Ethran leaned forward and brushed a finger over her chin, the sugary substance alighting along the digit as his eyes caught hers.

"Do you think she's trying to make fun of me with this fruit?" Skylla asked.

Ethran was very close, his face a hands length from hers as she stared into his blue eyes with tremors shaking her stomach.

"I think she might have other thoughts in mind" he answered, almost in a whisper.

Skylla nodded slightly and Ethran leaned further, his fingers lifting her chin as his lips pressed against hers.

Wind washed over skin, her bracers and choker tingling dully as Ethran's element and the magic of the temple diminished them. She kissed him back, fingers dropping the fruit as she wrapped her arms around his neck.

They fell together into the cushions, swirling air around them. The light shone through the glass figure of Shera, illuminating their souls as they slowly became one.

"What are you thinking?" Skylla asked.

She pressed against the wind-born, naked, the Ghost Moon casting a silver glow into the sanctuary from the windows, the twinkle of a millions bright stars a glittering court around it.

"Aspara are of the wind… and our thoughts change as quickly," he said.

Turning, she pressed her breasts against his chest, eyes seeking his in the twilight. He looked at the vault, one hand behind his head and the other trailing along the small of her back.

"I don't know what that means…" she said.

He looked at her, face pale in the moonlight, saying, "Tell me about your cargo?"

She sat up slightly, "What?"

"I want to know what's on Kaleb's ship."

Reaching out, she found her top and held it across her chest as she shook her head.

"You can't be..." she whispered.

He sat up, "Serious? I am, and I thought you were as well."

She shook her head, speaking more to herself "This was only about the cargo,"

He grabbed her wrist and she fought him but he pulled her close, wind whipping around them and her choker burning her neck.

"No, this was about us, about the Enlightened... I thought you understood that?" he said.

She relinquished a moment, her eyes searching his.

He said, "Skylla, your captain carries something dangerous, something from a time when this city still kept a yoke on the necks of our kind and Samayan tome mages worked magic with little other purpose than our extinction."

She shook her head but he continued, "What happened here, between us, was only another step in your journey to find the next world... your true world."

"Journey..." she whispered, "Step..."

Pulling away, she grabbed her coat and threw it around her shoulders. Above, the kind face of Saint Shera mocked her as she walked from the hall, the doors swinging wide as the chill of the spring night enveloped her.

Ethran called after her, but Skylla kept moving. Her bare feet chilled on the flags as she came to the rail of the court. Above, the stars above where like pinpricks in a black velvet heaven and the Blood Moon shone in red fury over the horizon in the north. Below, the low country stretched out in shadowed glory, mountains spilling into foothills, and then opening to plains beyond.

*What have I done?*

She wrapped her arms around her shoulders, the wind coming up the mountainside to whip at her hair and draw tears from the corners of her eyes.

"Skylla!" Ethran called again, this time from the doors of the church.

She didn't turn, her stomach twisted in knots and the sweet taste of the night's bliss now turned to ash upon her tongue.

Minutes passed, the sound of Ethran's feet behind her bringing a shudder to her torso. His shadow stepped to the rail, hands reaching out to feel the long the smooth curve of the stone.

"I'm sorry," he said.

She didn't reply.

"I guess I've been fighting too long... and sometimes I get careless."

*No! I was the one who was careless.*

"It's just that I've seen what the Samaya are capable of, seen the destruction, and I know you can't understand it, but if you'd just give me a chance I'll show you."

"I think you've shown me enough," she said.

He sighed, several minutes passing before he spoke again, "Come back inside, you'll freeze out here and whatever you think of me, believing that I'd want to see you come to harm can't be on that list."

She ground her teeth but turned and walked back to the church, Ethran beside her. They entered, the hall no longer filled with food or comfort. Instead it looked as old and grey as the rest of the city.

"I don't think Shera is too happy with me either..." Ethran observed dryly.

Skylla collected her meager clothes, dressed, and then moved to a wall where she sat with her gun across her knees. Ethran did the same, a few feet away, the tranquil kindness of the early evening's silver light replaced by the power of crimson inside the chamber, Shera's lovely face now hard and wreathed in bloody flame.

*Forgive me. I thought I knew what I was doing, but I see I've been as foolish as ever.*

She bit at the corner of her mouth.

*Kaleb was right all along but I was blinded by the beauty and romance of a world I didn't understand, and now it's probably too late.*

Closing her eyes, she leaned her head against the cool stone and tried to calm her breathing, the call of a night bird playing outside.

From somewhere in the vault a voice whispered, "*The wind is a terrible bedfellow but a man of conviction will never leave you cold...*"

She opened her eyes.

"Did you hear that?" she asked.

Ethran looked around, "What?"

She turned to him, his handsome face not as flawless as it had seemed when they'd entered.

"Hear what?" he asked again.

Shaking her head, she closed her eyes and leaned back once more. "Nothing," she muttered. "It must have just been the wind."

# CHAPTER FOURTEEN

## *KALEB*

*If only Mya were with us I could see about getting all the women in my crew killed in one fell swoop.*

*Saints! Why has it come to this? Arvilla deserved more than the end I led her to, more than some meaningless random bullet that struck a vital point. Here I am, alive, and beside me she is wrapped in a bundle of cloth, just like so many others I have known over the years.*

*How is it that a man can walk into battle half a hundred times and come out unscathed while soldiers die around him by the dozen? What fickle hand of fate keeps stray bullets at bay, diverts the eye of a waiting sniper, or wards bombards from their deadly purpose for one man but not another?*

*Why am I so untouchable? Is it because I've nothing to lose? Do only those who care about life, who have family or loved ones, draw death to them like moth to flame?*

*I cannot say, but I know the grey oblivion inside me grows. The fertile garden of life I tried so hard to foster these past five years withers with each passing hour.*

*Soon, I fear I will be little more than a soulless automaton like the one I struck down today, a simple killing machine that wanders the world in search of its next victim…*

The sun rose among the black towers of the city, orange and vibrant as it burned away yesterday's snow into a silvery mist that crept about the buildings and settled in the darkened places of shadows.

Kaleb was first to rise, no sleep finding him during the long night. Stoneham was next, and then Doc Rose, and finally the rest of the company stirred as coffee brewed on a small fire kindled by the Quartermaster.

The crew toasted to Arvilla's memory, warmed themselves, ate a meager round of dry food, and then moved out of the hanger through a rear hatch. It led down a series of curved steps into a sparsely decorated central atrium. The circular node, set with stone benches, withered trees, and four dried fountains was a pinwheel from which a dozen other enormous hangers spun out. At the garden's center stood a statue, the ground around it set with bronze veins in the marble that created a giant compass.

Kaleb approached the statue, a plaque on the stone beneath reading, 'The glory of the sky is ours, and we are the ones who will keep it: General Jessep T. Malett'

Kaleb looked up, the figure rising above forged in green copper and looking skyward. He was tall and majestic, and wore an expression of determination along with his Air Captain's trench and hat.

"You think he really looked like that?" Stoneham asked.

"I've seen pictures, and yes, it's a pretty good likeness, although this one carries a bit more nobility than was probably present in his soul."

Stoneham laughed and then turned to look at the huge buildings around them. All where enormous, easily fifty feet tall, half glass. Eight of them held the huge double doors while four had smaller entries and carried the markings of administration or barracks.

"It's your pick, Captain," he said.

Kaleb pointed to a triple-domed hanger directly across from the one they'd stayed the night. "Let's take the north. Perhaps more luck lies there."

They marched on, up a long flight of marble steps, through an empty guard post, and then pulled open a smaller access door that was cast inside the two larger gates.

The hanger was in better shape than the last. All three smaller domes topping it were still intact, and they broke the structure into a trio of units, each connecting a small metal plank and chain bridge to connect them. On the far side, some four hundred feet away, stood two other doors framed in glass that looking onto the open sky.

The company entered as a group. The first unit stood empty except for a handful of work stations and fabrication nodes, but the second held a huge, forty-foot tower of fabric hanging from a thick chain at the top of the glass dome. Below the fabric lay a large box with what looked like a gas ship engine turned on a vertical plane above it.

"What do you make of that?" Stoneham asked.

"That perhaps our luck is about to change," Kaleb answered.

"Captain?"

Turning, Kaleb motioned to the stations around them. "Check these, then move on, same teams as yesterday."

*Same as yesterday, less one...*

The crew spread out, Stoneham shaking his head as Kaleb walked over the metal bridge that crossed a twenty-foot drop into some kind of reservoir. When he reached the large box beneath the fabric, he ran a hand over the metal frame, rivets sunk into place along the corners and window frames cut into two panes so that they could be slid open.

The thing was ten feet by ten, with two four-foot wide windows on three sides and a single door on another that was flanked by two smaller glass panes.

He looked up, the fabric above was a mass of stitches and dust, although at such a close proximity it could have been a leather membrane rather than spun cloth.

"Observation balloon," he whispered.

Parish and Greylin moved past him, the two men carrying their rifles pointed forward as they made their way toward the third unit.

"Keep your eyes open," he ordered brusquely.

They nodded, and he took another long walk around the box before Tolbert came up to him, Lancaster lagging back as he looked over the side of the bridge at the darkness below.

"Nice balloon," Tolbert said.

"You think?" Kaleb asked.

Tolbert nodded, "Give me a boost and I'll take a look at the heater."

Kaleb put his hands together in front of him, squatted, and Tolbert stepped into his palms, placing his hands on the Captain's shoulders as his commander gave a lift.

The Mid-Tech grabbed the lip at the top of the box and pulled himself onto the roof. Kaleb waited below, Lancaster coming up to stand next to him.

"Will it fly?" the bosun asked.

Kaleb shrugged, "Not without a cell I'd think."

Lancaster nodded, and Tolbert looked over the edge, his face covered in dust.

"She's still in pretty good shape, but there's no cell in the slot."

Yogo came across the bridge and rested Arvilla's body on the floor near the box, Doc Rose beside him and Stoneham bringing up the rear.

"Anything?" Kaleb asked.

They shook their heads and Kaleb nodded. He turned to say something to Stoneham when a flashing red light and a warning buzzer sounded from the third unit.

Stoneham cursed, and above them Tolbert yelled down, "I think they found power!"

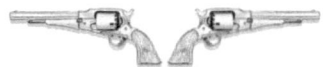

Kaleb ran across the second bridge as a machine that looked like a pile driver smashed down into the metal floor of the hanger. The reverb of the strike shook the walls and a tremor ran through the floor.

"What in the name of the Saints?" Stoneham yelled ahead of him.

Parish and Greylin stood by the machine, their faces ashen and eyes wide.

"We were just looking for cells!" Parish said.

The central hammer rose up again, heat coming from the wide legs on either side of it and steam rising out of the central core.

"Captain!" Tolbert yelled. "There!". Kaleb looked back just as the driver struck again, the impact actually raising his feet off the floor an inch.

"The locker! Look at the markings!" Tolbert was screaming and pointing.

Kaleb ran past the two youths, Stoneham climbing on the pile driver's leg toward a control box. Beyond the pile driver, another machine sat, this one a gunner's swivel mount that housed a now-outlawed Elemental Zoner.

Kaleb ran past it, eyes searching the edges of the unit until he found a large locker on the west side, the armada symbol for elemental power painted on the front in faded red.

The driver fell again, some glass panes in the dome above shattering and a shower of twinkling shards falling down around the machine.

Kaleb kept moving, hand grabbing the front of the locker but it held against his pull.

"Damn!"

He pulled out his pistol, got to the side of the handle and fired. The bullet ricocheted off the metal and the handle was twisted but unbroken.

He fired again, the driver striking right after. The handle still held and he kicked it twice, Yogo coming to stand next to him.

"Let me try, sir," he said.

The youth grabbed the handle in both hands and twisted until his face was red as an apple and the cords in his neck stood out. The bolt groaned, whatever damage the two shots had done sufficient for Yogo to pry it open a quarter inch.

The young crewman let go, a gasp of air filling his lungs, but Kaleb patted him on the back before moving to a work station.

"Find a pry bar!" Kaleb yelled.

The driver stuck again, more glass falling down. Parish screamed as a shard entered his shoulder, having fallen a hundred feet from the dome above.

Kaleb was still rummaging through a maintenance closet when Yogo came back to the locker and jammed a metal rod into the small hole. He gave a great grunt, his boot coming up to press against one door as he pulled the rod away.

The lock pinged open, the door swinging wide and Yogo sprawling on the ground as another driver strike pounded the floor.

Kaleb raced to the open locker, hands reaching inside as he drew forth a two foot cylinder that pulsed with blue light from a dozen runes cut in the surface.

He turned, yelling toward the second unit, "Azure?"

From the top of the box Tolbert shook his head and yelled "No, crimson!"

Yogo was up and standing beside him, his pack at the ready. Kaleb slipped the Azure Cylinder into the waiting bag and then reached again, spinning the long rods as he did so. Two Emeralds followed the Azure. Finally he found a Crimson rod and slid it out.

"Get this to Tolbert!" he said.

Yogo took it and bolted for the second bridge, more glass and even some metal tumbling around him.

Kaleb looked at Stoneham, who was standing atop one leg of the driver. The Quartermaster shook his head, yelling, "It's locked, I can't stop it!"

Nodding curtly, Kaleb called Greylin over. The youth came to a stop next to him and he loaded four Emeralds and three other Azure rods into the bosun's pack. Behind him, Stoneham slipped off the driver and helped the wounded Parish across the bridge.

"Get these to the box," Kaleb said.

Greylin nodded and sprinted away. Kaleb turned back to the locker, pulled five Crimsons, tucked them beneath his trench and looked back at the box. Yogo stood blocking his view, panting and holding his pack open once more.

Kaleb smiled, grabbed three more random cylinders, and then dropped all he carried into the waiting bag. With a last reach, he grabbed another Crimson rod and then turned toward Yogo.

"Go!" he ordered.

Yogo stood still, his green eyes staring at the side wall until Kaleb turned to follow his gaze. There, amid the shadow, something was moving quickly over the ground, antennae waving and wings buzzing.

Kaleb drew his pistol and fired, the huge insect sliding sideways but still coming. He fired again, this time striking it in the head and downing it.

"Let's go," he said.

Yogo nodded and the two of them started running for the bridge.

Stoneham met them on the span, his eyes wide and Lancaster at his side.

"This place crawls!" he yelled.

Kaleb looked behind him, dark shapes skittering all over the glass around the doors at the sky side of the hanger.

"How long?" Kaleb asked.

Stoneham shook his head, "Tolbert thinks ten minutes."

A curse escaped Kaleb's lips and he pulled the Crimson cylinder from his trench.

"There's an Elemental Zoner back there. I'll see about holding them," he said.

Stoneham grabbed the cylinder from his hands, "Like hell you will... Sir."

Kaleb tried to take it back but Stoneham shoved him aside and bolted for the waiting cannon, Lancaster right at his heels.

"Get that balloon going!" Stoneham yelled over his shoulder.

"Saint's speed," Kaleb whispered in benediction.

He broke for the box, Yogo beside him. Doc Rose was already inside, Arvilla's body and the wounded Parish prone beside him as he worked at the wound.

Above, Tolbert called, "Captain, I can get this thing lit, but we need the dome open!"

Kaleb grabbed Yogo's bag away from him and then tossed it inside the box.

"Come with me," he said.

The former apprentice followed, Kaleb running to the side of the unit and the tangle of stations there. The pile driver struck once more, and glass nearer the second unit started to break free and fall. Shots rang out from the third unit, Lancaster's rifle finding targets on the interior.

Moving boxes aside, he followed a series of pulleys and chains until they met up at a huge double-sided crank. Beside it sat a button, which he pushed but nothing happened. He threw a lever beside it, then pulled out a pin from the crank and turned to Yogo.

"You take the left," he said.

They began twisting the crank, and above there was a mighty groan of metal that was drowned out by a vacuous discharge from the third unit. A blaze of orange-gold light lit the hanger, and a chorus of hissing split the air.

Kaleb grunted against the crank, the chains taught. Yogo did the same beside him but it didn't budge.

*Saints give me strength…*

The pile driver struck again, the building shuddering and a shower of rust falling from the second dome. The crank gave an inch and then – slowly – started moving.

*Thank you.*

Kaleb threw all his strength into turning the crank and above them a piece of the dome started to slide beneath the rest. Like a man waking from slumber, the roof slowly opened to the sky as Lancaster and Stoneham continued to unleash hell at the front of the hanger.

# CHAPTER FIFTEEN

## *SKYLLA*

*I am a fool to believe this world held any fate for me other than that of a slave, be it bound by bands to the Samaya or played like a set of cards in the hands of the Enlightened.*

*It's a hard thing, realizing your true place and bowing your head to that unforgiving destiny. I now walk alone in my shame and betrayal. The one thing I ever knew, ever believed in, and I turned my back on it at the first opportunity presented.*

*Kaleb... what have I done?*

Skylla walked in the dawn light, the sky a clear blue and the dew burning away as heat flowered along the slopes from the valleys below. Her boots clanged against metal, her legs ached, and she watched as the hanging estates fell away beneath them as they crested the final switchback to the surface of the plateau and the black towers of the main city.

"We've made it to the top... now we just need to find your captain," Ethran said.

She didn't answer, silence her only comfort.

*My Captain... the one you wanted me to scathe with my words before I betrayed him with my body...*

Her eyes watched his back, but the Enlightened rarely turned back to look at her, instead keeping his distance as he picked his way among the buildings.

They moved on, up into a collection of markets, through a governmental building, and into an old carriage station. There was no sign of recent passage or residential life on the trail, as Ethran stopped at intervals to check some unseen detail and Skylla stared hollow-eyed at nothing.

"I can't find any sign of their passing this way. The city is pristine other than an occasional stray animal," he said.

She nodded and he took off his hat, fingers running through his dark wavy hair.

"You're going to have to talk to me at some point," he said.

"I am talking to you," she answered without emotion.

He laughed, saying, "Skylla, you're young, very young compared to me, so I wish you'd trust me when I tell you I meant what I said last night."

She didn't look at him, saying, "I may be young, but I've known you all of a week, and Kaleb, the man who saved me from the slave markets, has been loyal to me for three years. If you expected me to betray him so easily, all your years haven't added up to a great deal of wisdom."

He shook his head, "But he bought you! Can't you understand he's just taking care of an investment?"

The choker burned her neck and her bracers sent shocks along her arms, the smell of the ocean welling up around her as she turned on him with eyes dark. "I'd hold your tongue where the Captain is concerned..."

Ethran raised his hands in placation, "Fine."

He turned to walk on, the wind twisting around him and the air cool. She followed, boots kicking at random pebbles along the avenue as her fingers slid absently along the trigger of her gun.

*I've got to find a way to make this right.*

Only the wind answered her thoughts, the streets twisting on as an hour passed with Ethran going in and out of buildings along the way. He was coming down the steps of another buttressed structure when a tremor reverberated through the plateau and they both froze.

"Earthquake?" Skylla asked.

Ethran shook his head, "No."

They paused a moment, Ethran walking slowly in a circle before the shudder rippled along the street again.

"Kin Hammer," he said to himself

"What?"

He looked up, his eyes filled with fear.

"Someone is setting off a Kin Hammer!"

She shook her head, "I don't know what that means."

"It's a pre-war device that sends a sonic pulse through the ground. Kin hate it, and it drives them out of the earth. The Samaya used it to capture them intact."

"Why would someone be using one here when there are no Kin left?"

"I have no idea, but there are other things just as sensitive to such a device inside this plateau and there's only one other person we know might be here."

Her face grew pale. "The Captain."

"He must have no idea what he's doing," Ethran said.

"We have to warn him!"

He nodded, "Then we'd better hurry because the nest will have already felt that reverb and I'm sure they're none too happy."

They ran down an empty street, old air-ship hangers rising up before them as they broke into a circular garden. She raced down seven flights of steps and then up them again on the far side, her breath coming in great gasps. Ethran was always a dozen steps ahead, the Aspara slipping like wind across the ground before her.

In the distance a pistol discharged.

*Kaleb you're here!*

Ethran opened the door to a hanger, the inside housed rotted tri-wing aircraft painted with black mountains on their tails and wings. Skylla followed, her nail gun in hand and sweat streaming down her face as they sprinted the length and burst out the far side, the sound of rifle fire coming from a hanger to their north.

"There!" he pointed.

The hanger was a tri-domed thing across from a lowered central garden. Around it a ring of swarming dark shapes already washed against the foundation like black waves.

"We're too late," she said.

He continued forward shouting over his shoulder, "Not quite. I'm in the open now."

She followed, Ethran decapitating several stray roaches along the stair until they reached the far side. He stopped below the hanger doors, a smaller door set within the larger covered with insects.

Inside, the Kin Hammer sounded again and the roaches hissed in unison. There was a flash of light and the sound of a heavy weapon thundered from the holes in the dome above.

"They have an Elemental Zoner!" Ethran exclaimed in surprise.

He raised his hand, wind swirling around him as he swung his fingers quickly from side to side. The air struck the roaches a physical blow, their bodies flung east and west away from the door like kernels of corn scattering on the stone pavers to either side.

"Go!" he yelled.

They both moved up, Ethran throwing the catch on the dented, scratched door before they both slipped inside and closed it behind them. Hisses and impacts followed, the Kin Hammer striking again and a blaze of orange fire jetting out on the far side of the hanger.

The first unit was empty, but a bridge connected it to the second platform where a half-full balloon waited with a large, windowed box below.

"You'd better go!" Ethran said.

He raised his hand and a burst of air struck a small collection of roaches that had just broken through the wall to their left.

Skylla moved, her boots ringing on the metal as she hit the bridge. Below her the sound of hissing rose up, the darkness boiling like a pot of tar. The Kin Hammer struck once more, the bridge swaying as she barely made it across, the balloon growing larger by the second as Tolbert nursed fire from the engine.

Above, the roof slowly opened and she saw Kaleb and Yogo working a crank at the far wall. A roach skittered out of the crevasse beside her and onto the second unit trailing oil from its legs as it started moving toward Kaleb's back. Skylla raised her gun and fired, the shaft pinning the thing to the ground with a distinctive ping.

Kaleb turned with eyes narrow and sweat streaming down his face. For a moment he relaxed, but Yogo continued to spin the crank and he was dragged back to his task.

She reloaded as the Elemental Zoner fired a swath of energy over the front of the third unit, roaches incinerating in droves as they poured unheeded through a half-dozen openings in the far side. Stoneham was on the weapon, Lancaster beside him firing away with his rifle at any strays that made it close to the swivel mount.

Greylin was defending the second bridge, the bayonet on his rifle slick with green blood as he punctured another roach crawling out of the oil near his position.

Skylla moved up next to the box, looked inside and saw Doc Rose working on an injured Parish.

"Skylla...?" Parish whispered.

Rose kept his head down, "She's dead, kid, stay with me now."

"No!" Parish bobbed his head back and forth, "She's here..."

Rose pressed on Parish's injured shoulder and the young man's eyes grew wide as he screamed.

"Nothing like a little pain to keep you on this side and away from ghosts," Rose whispered.

She ducked back out, looking to the first unit. Ethran was at the bridge, his arm waving about as he pushed wind around the platform and cast roaches in all directions. Behind him more insects pulled themselves out of the oil pit, the closest to him pinned to the floor as she launched another nail.

"Three minutes!" Tolbert yelled above her.

Kaleb turned, Yogo still pumping away at the crank until it locked and there was a boom from the vault above. Open sky, white clouds playing in the atmosphere, shown down on the top of the balloon, but a single chain still locked it to the roof.

Skylla looked over at Kaleb, who was studying the same problem. He turned and marched toward the second bridge, his pistol blasting another roach back into the oil pit along the way.

"Stoneham!" he yelled.

The Quartermaster turned, a wicked smile splashed across his face and wet hair clinging to his cheeks.

"Captain?"

Kaleb pointed to the top of the balloon, "The housing chain!"

Stoneham looked up, nodded, and then tapped Lancaster. The Bosun dropped his rifle and exchanged places with Stoneham as the elder man pulled the sniper rifle from his back.

The Kin Hammer struck again, this time the entire sky side of the hanger falling away, a hundred roaches going with it. The tremor threw Stoneham off his feet and he tumbled from the turret as it slid sideways.

Lancaster adjusted his angle of fire and broke off another blazing spray of death, roaches burned by the dozen but the newly opened hanger allowed too many more of the creatures inside.

"Fall back!" Kaleb ordered.

He fired another round from his pistol, Yogo and Greylin flanking him with rifles firing as they tried to keep the bridge clear of vermin.

Stoneham righted himself and came to a knee, and not bothering to look back as he pulled his rifle to his shoulder. Placing his cheek against the stock, he leaned his right eye into his ocular sight. Behind, Lancaster was screaming insults, the barrel of the Zoner glowing as he continued to fire unabated.

A single shot rang out, and the balloon's tether chain slid free, Stoneham smiling as he pulled the rifle away from his shoulder.

The Kin Hammer struck again, this time a huge piece of the floor gave way, metal twisting and bowing downward as part of the plateau broke free and slid into oblivion. Skylla grabbed hold of the box, and Stoneham lunged for the far side of the second bridge, his rifle sliding away as he caught hold of a support post.

Behind him the Zoner pitched awkwardly, the barrel rising high as Lancaster held on and released another blazing gout of energy through what remained of the third dome. He screamed, roaches pouring over the turret as it slid toward the edge, the metal floor buckling without the stone beneath.

"Caster!" Tolbert yelled from above.

The Zoner fell from sight, another blast of fire shooting skyward after it was gone and more roaches flowing into the building in a black tide.

Skylla turned to Ethran. The Aspara was still standing on the first bridge, arms raised and wind sweeping around his flapping coat and tangle of long hair. Beyond him, an even greater amount of roaches were being held back by a wall of wind, the creatures blown back again and again as they crawled over each other to get to the Kin Hammer.

Skylla screamed his name over the howl of the wind. He looked back, smiling, "I've got this, just get loaded!"

Behind her, Stoneham was crossing the bridge as the Kin Hammer struck again, whatever bolts holding the metal span in place collapsing with his added weight.

Stoneham tumbled but kept hold of the chain railing before he disappeared from her view. Kaleb dropped down, his torso hanging over the lip as Yogo grabbed his legs.

Greylin fell forward and pulled as Kaleb strained, both men heaving up until Stoneham appeared at the lip, his face ashen and his hands bleeding.

Skylla ran to them, helped Stoneham stand and he stared at her a moment before Greylin screamed.

A roach attached itself to the former brigand's left arm, oil spilling off it as blood squirted from the wound. Kaleb went for his pistol, but Yogo stepped forward and grabbed the things mandibles between his fingers, blood welling up from his palms as he tore the roaches grip loose and split the creature's skull in the process.

"Come on!" Tolbert yelled.

The Mid-Tech dropped to the ground as the box drifted off the ground and strained against its lower tether. Skylla fell back, Kaleb at her side as Yogo, Greylin, and Stoneham all brought up the rear.

She jumped in, the others following as the balloon dipped and the floor scratched against the platform. Tolbert jumped to a series of levers and threw one up, the engine above whirring as the box jumped.

"Ethran!" she called.

Going to the door, she looked out. The Aspara was still at the bridge, but he looked up at the balloon and waved, as sea of black swirling around him, the wind still playing with his coat and hair.

She whispered his name again, the balloon rising away as he clasped his hands together and a globe of wind held the roaches at bay around him. The Kin Hammer struck a final time, and another huge slide of rock broke free from the plateau, the bridge giving way, as did the second unit and the dome above it. She watched Ethran fall away with the rest of the building down into the two-thousand-foot abyss below.

Kaleb took her arm and brought her inside before sliding the door closed. The crew was collapsed on the floor of the cabin, all breathing heavily as they drifted up into the tranquil morning sky.

# CHAPTER SIXTEEN

## *KALEB*

*Somehow, she's come back. In my hour of darkness when all else seemed lost she appeared as a savior, like she always has, and now I sit, conflicted, unsure of how I can make her understand the emotions coursing through me veins.*

*With Arvilla I was too guarded, and now it's too late, her body wrapped in a shroud. I thought the same true for Skylla, but there she sits, drawn up tight and distant, but I could approach, I could offer words of gratitude, or joy, or so many things. Yet I sit here alone.*

*Am I so damaged? Have I lost so much in my life that even when provided a gift from the Saints I can't bring myself to accept it?*

*There is sadness in all this that's too profound to truly face. Instead, I'll turn away like I always do, watch from the distance and hope that something will shake me from this torpor, but if Skylla's return from the dead can't do it, then I'm not sure anything ever will…*

"He'll live," Doc Rose pronounced with relief.

Parish lay sleeping, his shoulder a mass of bandages and blood. Around the two sat the rest of the company, Tolbert maneuvering a series of controls, Yogo holding his bandaged hands over his knees, Greylin's glazed eyes touched with the milk of the poppy as he absently stroked his wounded leg, and Stoneham standing and staring out a window into the open sky.

Kaleb sat with his back against the cool metal wall. Across from him Skylla mirrored his position, her eyes downcast and her gun still clutched in her hands.

"Good work Doc," Kaleb offered reassuringly.

Rose wiped his hands on a handkerchief and adjusted his spectacles.

"Are you sure you're unwounded, Captain," Rose asked.

Kaleb nodded, "My wounds aren't something you've the skill to heal."

Skylla looked up, her eyes meeting his a moment before she went back to staring at her weapon.

"Well, we've a Gola for the other things," Rose said.

Kaleb stood, stretched, and walked to where Tolbert worked. The Mid-Tech had a small rod in his left hand and was waving it slowly over a glass plate.

"What do you make of her?" Kaleb asked.

"A fine craft, if a bit tricky in these winds, and don't forget our uninvited guest," Tolbert pointed north.

There, along the lip of the horizon grey clouds bled into the earth like a painter's brush had dragged them down in long uneven strokes.

"A storm," Kaleb grumbled, unsurprised.

"A nasty cell, too, from the look of it. Then again you said you wanted rain on this journey, right?"

"That was when we were on the ground, not ballooning over uncharted territory."

"Not to worry, Captain, we're making good time and I think I'll have her on the ground at the Tyger before the storm catches us."

Kaleb patted the man on the shoulder, choosing not to ask if the pilot had ever actually landed an airship before. "See to it, Mr. Tolbert."

Turning, he moved over to where Yogo sat, and knelt beside him.

"How are the hands?"

"The Doctor says they'll heal well enough," Yogo answered.

"Well, at least you'll be off deck duty until them, and I think the break is well-earned," Kaleb said.

"Sir, I can still work!" Yogo said.

Kaleb smiled and nodded, "Not to worry, we don't put people off the Tyger for injury, and after what you showed me on the plateau there's no doubt you've a place with us for a long time to come."

Yogo smiled, "Thank you, Sir."

Nodding, Kaleb moved on to Stoneham, both men staring out the window for some time. Below, the world drifted by, everything so tiny from their vantage. Streams cut the brown and green land, small clumps of hardy trees stood out, some already with leaves sprouting. Ruined settlements scattered about the landscape, their dark stone like a blight upon an otherwise virgin ground.

"Lancaster was a good man," Kaleb said.

"Yeah…we've lost a lot of good men recently."

"It's a tough life, always has been."

Stoneham shook his head, "Two dead on this little trip, two more at the Tyger, and three at the docks when we picked up this damnable cargo. Captain, I have to ask, what are we carrying?"

"Stoneham, you as much as anyone knows that kind of backward, what if, thinking leads to madness. Once you start blaming stuff on any one choice, it won't end well. It's not the cargo that got our people killed, it's a run of ill luck, the same we could have had carrying foodstuffs from Findalynn to Taux."

"Captain, only the Doc and Skylla have been with you longer than I have, but I do wonder if you really understand what you're asking of the ship? Crossing a deadzone is madness, and I won't believe that a food run across the Halo is in the same conversation as this quest."

Kaleb stared out into the sky, the thunderhead flashing in the distance.

"Maybe, but there's no going back now, so you'd better make peace with it because I've no room for those who second guess my decisions."

Stoneham nodded, pushed away from the window and sat down in a corner. Kaleb stood a while longer, the storm continuing to brew as the wind picked up before it and pushed the balloon ever southward.

Rain came down in sheets, Olaf, Stoneham, and Tolbert struggling to get the balloon stowed beneath the starboard nacelle as Kaleb and Skylla tied down the observation box on the deck.

Lightning split the sky and everyone ducked, water sloshing up around the pontoons as the river rose around them with a storm surge.

"She's down! Let's go!" Kaleb called.

Skylla nodded and the two of them ran to the deckhouse, slamming the door behind them. Water poured off their trenches, and their hair stuck to their foreheads.

"That's a nasty piece of work," Kaleb said.

Skylla nodded, "Yes, Captain. Do you want me to check the port repairs, make sure it's all holding?"

"Go," he said.

She went up the stairs to the bridge and he wiped water from his face.

"Again, Captain, I'm glad to have you home in one piece," Mya said as she drew back her curtain.

"It's not the time," he answered tersely.

Boots clanking against the stair, he made his way to the bridge, threw his coat on the navigator's chair and dropped into his seat.

"What say you, Mr. Gates?" he asked.

Morgan turned, a smile on his face, "Nice to have you back, Captain."

"Yes, yes, but can you steer us out of this mess?" he asked.

"Yes sir!"

Kaleb leaned over and called into the engineering tube, "Pascal, I'm going to need 5 REM."

"5 REM." Pascal repeated.

The ship lurched, turned, and Gates fought the helm until it righted course, the weather-eye showing the surging water coming directly at them from upstream.

"Slow and steady, Mr. Gates."

The Tyger crept forward, Kaleb watching the pontoons bounce as white-water splashed against them.

"8 REM, Pascal." Kaleb ordered.

"8 REM."

The ship picked up speed, the shore drifting by as Kaleb leaned back.

"How long till the next exit?" he asked.

Silence, Gates finally turning around as Kaleb sat staring at the weather-eye.

"Sir?"

"Nothing, Mr. Gates, just old habits. Keep us moving forward."

Gates turned around, and Kaleb looked back at Arvilla's station.

*Ghosts come back to roost...*

Doc Rose came up from the port deckhouse, a flask in his hand and a glow about his cheeks.

"Seems we're under way," he observed unnecessarily.

"Indeed, but I need some navigation help. Can you check a map?" Kaleb asked.

Rose nodded, pushed the wet trench off the station chair and sat down.

"What am I looking for?" he asked.

"The next probable river exit. Arvilla should have it marked but I'll need a time calculation versus our last location at 8 REM, assuming we're making that speed against this current."

"I'll do what I can, but it's been a long time," Rose said.

Kaleb waited, pulled out a watch from his vest and checked the time. *Ten minutes...*

"Looks like maybe twenty minutes," Rose said.

"You hear that Mr. Gates, the exit should be in another ten or twelve if you combine Doc and my calculations, so keep a lookout," Kaleb said.

"Yes sir."

The Tyger moved on, Gates taking her close to the starboard bank as the ruins of a town appeared, their dark shapes sprinkled along the shore.

"There!" Kaleb called out.

Gates adjusted the helm, the ship turning in the water and Kaleb yelling to Engineering, "Give me 10 REM and bring down the wheels!"

The ship shook, lanterns swinging above the work stations and the thunder booming directly above.

"Looks like nature isn't going to make this easy" Kaleb whispered.

Below, the sound of the wheels locking into place shook the ship, and Kaleb said, "Full ahead, Mr. Gates, let's get out of this water and onto some land."

The Tyger roared toward the shore, the wheels impacting the riverbed as the front of the ship slowly climbed upward.

They lost track of the horizon, only the grey sky showing before the weather-eye dropped back down and scattered trees and ruined building stood around them, the Tyger slowly running over everything in its path.

"Steady..." Kaleb ordered.

Lighting struck nearby, the weather-eye temporarily blinded before the world reformed and sheets of cutting rain continued to pour down from above.

"Keep her out of the worst of it," Kaleb said.

Morgan spun the wheel, the ship turning starboard, then port, and then starboard again until the ruins gave way to the open fields beyond, long grass moving like the waves of the ocean before them.

"Nicely done, Mr. Gates, now keep her steady. I'll be in my ready room."

Rose called after him, "Get some sleep, that's an order."

Kaleb shut the door to the small chamber behind the bridge, flopped into the cot hung against the wall and closed his eyes.

*Saint Siegfried, give me strength!*

In moments, he was asleep, as the Tyger crawled its way through the rain.

"You've been very glib since you appeared in the hanger, but now we've a calm moment so I'd like to talk about what happened." Kaleb said.

Skylla sat across from him in his stateroom, her body covered in tech denim and a wool sweater as she leaned easily against the front of his desk.

"I'm not sure what you're asking," she said.

Kaleb leaned back in his chair, the ship shuddering slightly as they moved over uneven ground and his brow furrowed.

"Skylla, you fell off a mountain."

She kept looking at her hands.

"I don't remember," she said.

He sighed, "You don't remember anything?"

Looking up, water pooling in the corner of her eyes and she worked her lips back and forth.

Finally, she said, "No, I don't remember the fall, just waking up behind a waterfall in a cave."

"With Ethran?"

"NO! I mean, he wasn't there, not yet, just a fire and then when he came back I told him I needed to find you so we went into the caverns looking for the old Kin mines."

"A dangerous business for an Aspara," he said.

She nodded, "Yes, he grew pretty weak, but when the roaches attacked, we made it to an old elevator and it brought us further up the plateau."

"So you knew about the roaches, that the pile driver would bring them?"

"Yes."

"And that's when you found the party?"

His First Mate did not answer.

"Skylla, this isn't like you. In all our time together we've never kept secrets," he said.

"He showed me the city, told me stories of the Enlightened and even had me pet a sky whale," she said.

"Romantic," Kaleb observed cautiously.

She was shaking her head, "Captain, he saved my life, and he was saying all the right things... and when he showed me the Church of Saint Shera..."

Kaleb sat like a statue and Skylla started to shake.

"It was... he... I thought..."

Her words faded as she tried to reach out to him but he drew back.

"Please, Captain!"

He shook his head, saying, "You've always been a free woman, Skylla, no matter what that choker or those bands say. I've no place to make accusations, but I do need to know if anything happened that could put this mission in jeopardy."

She shook her head, "After... he wanted to know about the cargo but I wouldn't tell him anything."

*Saints.... I'm going to throw up...*

"How did he know in the first place?" he asked.

"I don't know, but I'd guess he can sense the heavy elements," she answered quickly.

"And yet when he found us on the river I'm sure he'd been there for days, waiting. This stinks of some deeper subterfuge."

"Captain... I'm so sorry.

He held up a hand, "That's all. You can return to your post."

She blinked, a hand wiping at her eyes, "Captain?"

His jaw was set and he eyes hard, "Dismissed."

She got to her feet, head hung low, and walked to the door. For a moment she paused with her hand on the knob, started to speak but the words were lost deep in her throat. Turning the catch, she went into the hall, the door closing with a hollow sound behind her.

Kaleb sat, the lantern in his room guttering twice. He mouth was dry and he reached into the bottom drawer of his desk and drew out a bottle.

He uncorked it, poured a glass of amber liquid, and took a hardy swig.

A knock sounded on the door and he sighed, took another long swallow and called out, "Enter."

The door opened, Mya's black cloaks swishing into the room.

He shook his head, "Gola, I really don't have time for this…"

Mya reached up and pulled the veil from her face, the lacy covering falling away until he stared at her for the first time in more than three years. She looked so young, little more than a girl, her face pale and spotted with freckles across her petite nose and over her cheeks. The skin around her eyes was painted deep blue, and her lips were thin and coated in a shiny wax that made them glow.

"Gola, I said…"

She stepped forward, hand going to the folds of her skirt as she pulled the fabric open and revealed long ivory legs naked to where the last folds ended at her upper thighs.

He blinked, mouthed something unintelligible as she came around the desk and straddled him, legs falling over his and her hands coming up to cup his face. She kissed him, her smell like honey-jasmine and her lips tasting of strawberries.

The glass dropped from his fingers, shattered on the floor, but he grabbed her and paid the sound no mind.

She drew back enough to catch a breath, whispering, "I am yours, give me your pain that I may ease your burden."

He kissed her, the lantern flicking and the night turning hot even as a cool rain fell outside.

# CHAPTER SEVENTEEN

## SKYLLA

*E*verything I've ever wanted is no more. I thought I had it all in my grasp and now it's slipped away into ash and smoke.

I saw the hurt in his eyes, saw the betrayal and I swear to you that I never knew, never understood until now. Of course I'd dreamed, but what foolish girl doesn't about a man who is so dashing and honorable? He saved me from the life I led before, the servitude and the defilement. Why wouldn't I love him? I had no idea he fostered such feelings for me.

Still, I witnessed the look I've seen in others when their lives are shattered, when those they love are taken from them by circumstance or death.

I've wounded him grievously, and now I must carry that burden till the day I die. What hope have I now? What action can forestall the steady demise that will surely consume us until my sin finally sees me cast from the ship as the traitor I am?

Saint Shera, if you are there, I beg you to listen, to give your blessing to me that I might mend the damage I've done, that I might right the wrong and see this thing through so that I can serve the purpose for which I was conceived. That is the only prayer I can give, and I hope against hope that it is enough...

Skylla watched on the weather-eye as the Gola moved from the deck-house to the starboard quarters. The light from the captain's porthole was soon snuffed out, and the Gola did not return.

Upon the extinguishing of the light, she fled the bridge, Morgan calling after her as she climbed the stairs to the observation deck and released her meager dinner over the rail. Rain poured down, and off to the west beyond the rolling clouds the Ghost Moon waned, its large pale face sliding down the star-filled sky as the Blood Moon chased it and turned the world into a land of bloody shadow.

"I'll kill her" she whispered.

The smell of the sea poured into the night, the salty essence mixing with the mist that shrouded the ground and clung to her face in little drop-lets as the rain petered out.

She rubbed at her bracers, shocks traveling up her arms as she cursed, spat, and raged around the circular deck in a subdued tirade.

Thunder boomed in the distance, yesterday's storm having departed to the south with the coming night but a new and more powerful cell chasing its skirts from the north.

When the shocks ceased and her ire played out, she sank to the floor, eyes closing as she leaned into the smooth curve of the rail.

*I've got to control this! There is no one to blame but myself.*

She sat, the Tyger lumbering on over the plain as her thoughts mingled with dreams, drops of rain finally waking her.

The Blood Moon was hidden away, new clouds having turned the crim-son night to ebony. Skylla stood, more rain striking her until she raised her face and let the oncoming shower soak through hair and unfamiliar and heavy clothes alike.

The choker pulsed and the bracers tingled as she drew off her denims and other clothing until she stood naked in the downpour.

*Saint Shera, wash away my sins...*

Thunder boomed again, lighting sparking in terrible green bolts across the sky, but the water-born stood tall upon the highest point of the ship.

*Take me if you will or leave me reborn, one way or another I'll not be the same as I was when I came here...*

"Skylla?"

She turned, water pouring from her as Doc Rose walked up the stairs. For a moment they stared at each other, water dripping from Rose's crum-pled hat.

"He's with the Gola," she said.

Rose nodded and then waved her back down the stairs as he turned.

"I'll make you something to take the edge off and warm you up, but come down before you catch your death."

She stood for a moment in the rain, shuddered once, and then collected her clothes, the warm light of the bridge spilling out into the stairwell as Rose left the door open for her.

Kaleb sat in the Captain's chair, Skylla behind him at the navigator's station and Greylin holding down helm duty.

The weather-eye showed the windswept plain, little more than tangled grass, scattered trees, and baked earth that were now turned to a muddy bog in the incessant rains.

"Give me a position," Kaleb said.

"Four hundred miles west of Storm Lake, but less than two hundred to the Estyfyr River," Skylla said in the clipped tones of an officer offering a report to a superior.

Kaleb tapped his fingers on the chair, saying, "Forty hours if we keep this speed and course."

"The map indicates a settlement at the headwater, a place called Broken Branch," she offered.

"It's a way station, a caravan post for Mountainbacks and their drivers to resupply for journeys across the Soyuz veldt."

"Will we be stopping there?" she asked.

"The ship needs further repairs before we take on a lake, so yes, we'll be forced to stop I think."

"I'll get a more precise location when the moons rise, then we can adjust the helm accordingly," she said.

He rose from his seat, "Good, see to it."

She watched him take the starboard stair and then got to her feet, eyes searching the starboard deck as she counted away the seconds.

At eleven Kaleb appeared on the deck, hat atop his head as he crouched from the rain and ran to the quarters located beneath the nacelle.

"Looks like the Gola didn't snare you this time," she muttered.

"Ma'am?" Greylin asked.

She dropped into the Captain's chair, the seat still warm and the smell of him lingering around her.

"Nothing, just keep her steady."

Greylin went back to holding the wheel. At intervals, he'd shift his weight and gingerly rub his left thigh.

"How is the wound healing?" she asked.

"Very well, Ma'am. Doc Rose said other than a tale-worthy scar I should be no worse for wear."

"You've proved your worth since we picked you up in Findalynn. I suppose you deserve to impress a few tavern wenches at the next port."

"Thank you, Ma'am."

Time slipped past until she spoke again, "How long were you with the gang?"

"Ma'am?"

"The gang you attacked us with."

"Oh… three years, miss, but it wasn't my first one. I've lived most of my life trying to survive in the shadows in the slums. It's a war down there, and you either pick a side or pick at the leftovers."

"A tough life."

"No tougher than most I'd guess, unless you were born rich."

She nodded, "Findalynn is a terrible parent, but those who can survive her abuse without falling to madness tend to be stronger for it."

"Are you…" he trailed off.

"What?"

"Are you from Findalynn?"

"Originally, no. I was born east of the city, or so I was told, but I spent the better part of my life there."

"As a slave," he added. It was not a question.

She laughed, "Yes, as a slave."

"The Gola says slaves are lucky, that they don't have to take responsibility for their lives and thus don't have the worries of free men."

"Does she now?" Skylla said. "Have you visited with the Gola often?"

Greylin's cheeks flushed and he let his black hair fall down around his face.

"A few times, miss."

"Is she everything people say?"

Greylin's only answer was to take a sudden interest in the dials at his station.

"Silence doesn't become you, Mr. Sumner."

"Sorry, Ma'am, it's just I have nothing to compare it to."

"You're a handsome enough fellow, Mr. Sumner. Am I to believe you've never been with a woman until now?"

He nodded, "Ladies were for the leaders, miss, and I had many years to go before I qualified for one."

"What about brothels?"

"You need coin for those."

She sat a moment, a frown on her face before another dark shape slipped across the starboard deck toward the nacelle. The Gola was on the move.

"Bitch!" she hissed.

"Ma'am?"

"Hard to port Mr. Sumner!" she screamed.

He jerked the helm hard, the wheel spinning and the ship lurching sideways. On the starboard deck, the dark figure was thrown off its feet and slid through the rain until is splashed into the gravity-collected pool of rainwater at the rail.

"Ma'am?" Greylin asked.

"Nicely done, Mr. Sumner, it looks like we avoided a difficult obstacle there."

"I didn't see anything," he said.

"Well, that's why you have me to help you."

On the deck, the black shape stood, flung water from its hands, and slowly walked back toward the deckhouse.

Broken Branch was a small thing, no more than a collection of docks and two dozen buildings made of clay bricks and high-plains thatch. The Tyger made the port in the early morning, repairs beginning in earnest, while those of the crew lucky enough not to be needed, and well enough to leave the ship, spilling out into the streets in search of drink and company.

Skylla sat in a tavern along the shore, smoke filling the single room with a yellow haze and the smell of wet animals drifting in from the attached stable. Stoneham, Greylin, Gates, Branson, Doc Rose, Ugarth, and the Captain all sat in the common room, some tossing cards with locals in a game of Bannoq and others drinking and toasting as they told stories of those lost along the journey.

Kaleb sat alone, having raised a single glass to Arvilla before he fell into a dark and brooding mood beneath his hat.

The people of the town weren't much to look at, mountain-stock Kulds who must have migrated from the High Castles of Mistfin, their hair dark

and their faces flat. Most wore small curved blades and desert-tan clothing with heavy leather boots. They smelled of Mountainback musk.

Scattered among the locals sat a few river traders. These were men of the eastern shores, with pale skin and light eyes, most sporting mustaches and carrying fine revolvers.

Skylla took a drink, her eyes straying to Kaleb again as he sat next to Stoneham, where the Quartermaster occasionally leaned over to whisper something to him. The words would elicit a nod or a furrowed brow, but few words were spoken in return.

Somewhere further back in the haze a man played a lonely tune on a set of pipes, and a woman in gold skirts and bangles danced on a table, but few men partook of the visual delight.

"Nice night for a roll, don't you think?" a strange voice asked.

She looked up from her seat, a tall easterner with a burgundy coat and high black boots stood next to her.

"Piss off," she said.

He smiled, a scar running down his left cheek turning red.

"That's no way for a trout-lipped Enlightened slave to talk to a man of Tiefon," he said.

She went for one of her knives but he grabbed her hand, his fingers like iron fastenings.

"Not so fast..." the stranger began.

"I'd back away," Kaleb said from two tables away.

The man looked up, his hand trailing down to his pistol, but Kaleb drew first and without hesitation.

A shot rang out, then another, the tavern gravely quiet as the stranger fell back and a man seated at a table nearby slumped across the top spilling drinks. An un-holstered pistol clattered to the floor beneath his chair.

Kaleb stood, his revolver smoking in his right hand and his left covering the hammer.

"Does anyone else have issues with my slave?" he asked.

Silence reigned.

He nodded and sat back down. Stoneham, who had barely had time to clamber from his bench, sat back down abruptly. Skylla's heart pounded as she looked down at the dead eyes of the man in burgundy.

Steadying herself, she took another drink, let the music come back to life and then got to her feet. Ugarth stood as well, the gambler collecting his winnings and rushing to catch her as she made the door.

"An escort, Ma'am," he said.

"Do you really think I need it?" she asked casting an eye back at the dead.

He smiled, "I was talking about me."

She shook her head, "As you will."

They moved outside, the rain having lessened since their arrival and now only a misty drizzle that filled the air with fog.

"He likes to send a message, doesn't he?" Ugarth said.

"It's the wastes, the only law is that which you make yourself, and he's pragmatic when it comes to the crew."

"Pragmatic. That's a new one. So killing two men to prove a point is pragmatism?"

"If they were left alive, it might set something in motion that could cost his crew later."

"No one can know that," Ugarth said.

"True, but he does know that dead men can't hire assassins, collect allies, or kill with a long-range rifle."

Ugarth shook his head, "Are you sure that's all there is to it?"

She passed a Mountainback stall, the great hairy beasts twice the size of a prairie wagon, with long faces and lips that constantly moved in a rhythmic chewing dance.

"What are you getting at?" she asked.

He took her hand, and she stopped.

"When we get to Tiefon and make this score, I'm going to leave the crew. I've seen what's happening between you and the Captain, and I want to ask for your title. If he sells you, I'll set you free."

She stared at him, finally saying, "You can't be serious?"

"I'm dead serious. I knew there wasn't a chance of this before you went to the mountains, but once you returned I asked around. The Captain has finally taken up with the Gola, and I've seen the way you two act toward one another. Something has changed, and I think he might take the offer, assuming you'd come with me."

"If you had my title, I'd have no choice but to come with you."

He shook his head, "No, like I said, I'd free you, but I've wanted... I mean, I've come to respect you this past eight months and I thought we might..."

She raised a finger, pointed it directly in his face.

"A rich pay out and some cheap compliments aren't enough to buy me, not my body, and not my loyalty, Ugarth, and you had better remember that."

He took a step back and she turned on her heel and marched back to the ship, a Mountainback blowing a great call behind her.

*Foolish gambler. What does he think, and how can he know how big our payout will be?*

# CHAPTER EIGHTEEN

## *KALEB*

*Do you think me a killer or do you think me a fool? Does it really matter in the end? Only Saint Siegfried will decide my final fate. Over the years I've learned the hard way that if you command, you must make hard decisions, and I've done so again.*

*That is the key of it, knowing when to choose the hard road versus the simple, when to show weakness and when to show strength. It was the way with those men, but the specifics are for me to decide, and the decision is made in an instant without a weighty council debating the rights and wrongs of things.*

*The Gola you ask? I hear you thinking it, asking in the silence, but I have no answer to give other than life brings what it does. It wasn't something I planned, but now that it's happened I've got to deal with it just like everything else.*

*That can wait till Tiefon, however. The city is a place of endings and beginnings I think, but only time will truly tell...*

Brandon Pascal, Mage-Tech, sat on a wooden support hung from the port rail of the Tyger, goggles over his eyes and an elemental brand in one hand. Light flashed, the repairs to the nacelle having made dramatic progress over the past two days as the rain dwindled and the late spring sun began to bring life to the plain beyond the little town.

*Good work, Brandon, you always keep my Tyger going, and for that I owe you...*

Yellow flowers bloomed along the shore as green grass slithered at their base. Nesting birds flew in the tranquil sky, migrations bringing them home and the warmth of spring taking command from the winter season.

Skylla came around the ship's side, approaching him as he oversaw Pascal's work. "Sir," Skylla said.

Kaleb didn't turn, his eyes still on the side of the ship.

"Skylla."

"You wanted to see me?" she asked.

He sighed, "Yes, walk with me."

She followed as he walked into the tall grass west of the ship, the town drifting away down the slope. A breeze drifted up, her violet hair catching in it and flittering around her face before she pulled it back and wove it into knot behind her head.

"There have been many unforeseen circumstances along the way," he said.

She didn't reply, and he finally stopped his march, the meadow around them alive with insects and decorated with white and gold flowers.

"Have you sensed the rains?" he asked.

"They're retreating, the warm air from the east bringing summer into the fold."

He nodded, "I feared that, my timeline off by more than a week, and with this season that's sometimes all it takes. I know we can make it across Storm Lake, but once there the journey ends, unless..."

"Captain?"

He turned to her, his hand slipping inside his vest as he pulled a slender gold rectangle from a chain on his neck. A breath caught in her throat and she backed up a step.

"I think we can make the crossing from the lake to the headwaters of the Mitrik River if you can keep the cargo wet."

She shook her head, but he continued, "To do that, I'll have to remove the bracers and choker."

The wind picked up, and he watched her as she stared at the rune key.

"I've trusted you with my life for three years, Skylla, and you've never disappointed me. I know what happened with Ethran. I even think I understand it, but I've got to put that behind us so we can move forward. Do you understand?"

"Captain... I..." Skylla could not find the words.

He reached out, surprisingly gentle as he took one of her hands and ran the rune key over the bracer. There was a flash of white light, and the oricalcum broke along her forearm into a series of teeth, the skin beneath pale and sickly.

She rubbed her wrist, ran her fingers over the skin and then looked up at him.

He continued, "We live in a cruel world, you and I, and I know what I want to give you will only lead to death, but perhaps you can savor the freedom and make what choice you will along the way."

She nodded and he placed the key on her other bracer, pausing until it fell into his waiting hand.

"Turn around," he said.

She did so and he closed the distance until he nearly pressed against her, the smell of her hair like the sea on a summer's day. Slowly, he ran the key down the back of her neck, the choker releasing as she sucked in a deep breath.

The air around them changed, the smell of the deep sea, of untold fathoms rose up as she turned to look at him. Her eyes were radiant emerald and her hair hung damp and straight as the knot gave way and her hair spilled like a violet wave down her back and shoulders.

"I won't disappoint you..." she whispered.

He nodded, and she leaned against him, a tingle of energy drifting through him as the hairs on the back of his neck stood on end. He reached out, held her, his heart racing in his chest as he stroked her damp hair and felt the tides of another world drift around him.

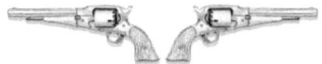

Storm Lake was so large it looked like an ocean where the Tyger slipped out of the Estyfyr River into its placid waters. Two days had passed since Broken Branch, the town having quickly turned into a hollow-eyed place where the trigger-happy captain's crew was avoided.

The men Kaleb shot were buried, a local man providing last rights to Saint Amanda with promises of their souls going into the everlasting light.

Now Kaleb stood on the observation deck, Stoneham beside him and the wind cutting across the waves from the east.

"She seems happy," Stoneham observed cautiously.

"Wouldn't you be?" Kaleb asked.

"I suppose, but really what have you given her?"

"A choice, which is all have to offer her, but after three years I think she's earned it."

Stoneham nodded, "Only you can know that, so I trust your decision. Still..."

"Still what?"

"Still, a better question might be why you killed those men in Broken Branch?"

"You saw what happened," Kaleb said.

"Yeah, I saw it, and I've also come to know you very well over the course of these last few years, and as far as I'm concerned you pulling your pistol has always been a last resort. In that fight, if you can call it that, there wasn't much in the way of a peaceful negotiation."

"He went for his gun and one of his comrades had already drawn his."

Stoneham laughed, "There's something you are not telling me."

Kaleb shrugged, "If I'm not, then it's for your own good."

They stood a moment, light playing along the waves in a shimmering ripple of gold, few clouds left in the sky after the departure of the spring rains.

"Who were they?" Stoneham said.

"Does it matter?"

"It does if I'm to help protect the crew and the ship. Otherwise how will I know what to look for?" Stoneham asked.

Kaleb sighed, finally saying, "I can't be sure, but like you I don't play with the lives of the crew. The leader had a thin waxed mustache, something not worn in either Dragmarsh or Tiefon, and they all carried Taux-forged sidearms. If that wasn't odd enough in these parts, the leader had a Garin Light Cavalry knife in his belt. The white horse on the pommel was a sure tell of his service."

"Garin agents?" Stoneham asked. "They'd be on the far side of the world if so."

"Exactly, which made me question what brought them to Broken Branch, other than to wait for us to show up at the closest port of call to Storm Lake along the wastes."

"By the Saints, Captain, again I have to ask: What are we carrying?"

"Something Garin doesn't want us to deliver, I can promise you that."

Stoneham looked down at the deck, the boxes tied down and covered with a tarp. Branson stood close by, his rifle slung over his shoulder and his cap drawn down over his eyes.

"I don't know. I still don't understand how they could have known which route we would take."

Kaleb sighed, "Well, there's only one way I can think of."

"A spy?" Stoneham asked, incredulous.

"Only time will tell."

Kaleb turned and left the deck, his coat trailing behind him as he took out a cigar and lit it.

*Only time will tell...*

The Tyger lurched as it rose out of the water, the eastern shore of Storm Lake a pleasant grasslands that housed a few remote farmsteads. The land was tranquil and green, life having crept back into the soil and hardy folk reclaiming the territory in the century since the great war.

Two children, cane poles in their hands, watched and cheered as the ship crept from the waves. Kaleb smiled at them from the bridge.

"Looks like someone is happy with our arrival into Tiefon lands," Kaleb said.

Morgan laughed and Skylla said, "Indeed, captain, and I'd better head to the deck to be sure we keep it that way."

She went down the port stair and Kaleb watched her walk across the deck to relieve Branson, her hands going out to run across the tarp.

*Keep them wet, Skylla, or this will be a very short portage over land...*

"What's that about?" Doc Rose asked the Captain.

He was at navigation with Greylin, a collection of charts, books, and instruments lying around them on the desk.

"Branson can't be there thirty-two hours a day, nine days a week, Doc," Kaleb answered.

Rose shook his head and then went back to his instruction, his lessons spilling over Greylin as the young man scratched his head and took notes. The Tyger started an easy roll, several small trees crushed beneath the pontoons as it moved from the shore.

"Keep her at 5 REM," Kaleb called to engineering.

"Aye, captain," Pascal replied.

The weather-eye opened up, the country growing broad and wide before them as Mya came from the starboard stair, a cup of tea in her hand.

"I thought you might be able to use this," she said.

He took the cup and she let her fingers slide against his. "If there is anything else?" she whispered invitingly.

"This will be all," he said.

She bowed, the smell of honeysuckle drifting around her as she withdrew to the stair. He turned and watched her go, the pace of his heart quickening and his mouth dry until he took a drink of the tea.

It was rich and sweet, the aroma easing his mind as the ship moved on, a game of pig-ball breaking out on the starboard deck.

He watched the three-man teams kick the ball around the deck, Olaf and Stoneham serving as team captains as they tried to bloody one another with the heavy ball.

"I've seen them play Ulama in Taux and its pretty rough, even compared to the Findalynn pig-ball version." Morgan said.

"Do tell, Mr. Gates, I never knew you were into sports?" Kaleb said.

"I'm not, but I do like to take a bet now and then," he said.

Kaleb watched him a moment, sipping the tea. The boy was young, black-haired and slim, with eyes dark and a ready smile on his face.

"I thought you were from Ebontra?" Kaleb asked.

"I am, Captain, but I shipped out at twelve aboard the Bronze Star and they spent two weeks in port at Taux every other month."

"Must have been some good times, but I hear the city is ghost-infested if you believe the sailor's tales," Kaleb said.

Morgan laughed, "Well, I can tell you I saw nothing while there, although I did feel like the city's ancient carvings did turn to look at me on occasion, but it was probably just shadows."

Kaleb nodded, took another drink and then lowered his glass as he focused on the weather-eye.

"Mr. Gates," he prompted.

"I see them Captain, what should I do?" Morgan asked.

Kaleb sat up, five men having come into view on the plain, their long-coats whipping around them in the wind and wide hats and scarves covering their faces.

"Keep her steady," Kaleb said.

The ship moved on, Skylla running up the port stair as they drew closer to the figures.

"Captain! I sense..." she trailed off.

The weather-eye focused in, the men among the tall grass holding no weapons but hammer, blade, and bow.

"Enlightened," Kaleb finished.

"Pascal, full stop!" he ordered quickly.

The ship slowed, Morgan engaging the brake and the Tyger groaning. By the time they stopped, the Enlightened were less than four hundred feet from the ship. Their leader took two steps closer before he pulled of his scarf.

"Ethran..." Skylla whispered.

"Damnable Saints!" Kaleb cursed.

He got to his feet but Skylla drew close and grabbed his arm. "Captain, let me talk to him, please."

He looked from her to the face displayed on the weather-eye then back again. "I don't think that's a wise decision."

"Captain, if those are Enlightened out there, it's the only decision. Let me try to settle this without bloodshed," she said.

"That won't happen."

Her eyes flared green, the smell of the depths rising up in the bridge. "Maybe not, but at least you'll know you tried, which is more than you can say for the men in Broken Branch."

He shook his head, "One day, Skylla, you'll come to realize..." He trailed off, leaving the thought unfinished.

She stared at him until he finally nodded, "Go, but be wary, they've come on a purpose and no matter what he says, that purpose isn't you, and we'll not give it up without a fight.

# CHAPTER NINETEEN

## SKYLLA

*I've come this far and begged for a purpose, Saint Shera, and now it seems you've provided it, and a grand one it is indeed. I swear to you that I thought I'd seen the last of him, but I should have known a fall couldn't kill him, just as it didn't when he saved me... a situation I've come to question more and more as I think about the strange wind that tore me from the rock as I tried to bridge that high mountain gap.*

*What kind words will he say, what apologies will he attempt this time, or will he even try to conceal his true nature? If I've learned anything, it's that a war still rages between my people and the Samaya and it will not end until only one race is left standing.*

*Now I've got to make the choice, side with my captors or go with my people, people whom I can't trust or identify with. Still, at least I am free to make that choice, a freedom provided to me by a man willing to not only kill for me but also risk his own life in my defense – the man who should be my enemy. So I ask you, who has the honor in this fight: the subjugated deceivers or their honorable masters?*

*You have tasked me no small thing, Shera, but I will do what I can to make you proud...*

Skylla walked across the ground, the tall grass waving around her, touching her legs and looking like a green ocean in the gentle breezes.

Ahead, Ethran came on, his partners holding back, as did the crew of the Tyger. Only Kaleb left the ship to stand beneath her starboard shadow.

"Skylla," Ethran said.

"Ethran, you look well," she replied cautiously.

"As do you. I must say I'm happy to see that you're finally free, because it was much easier to find the ship once I discovered your elemental scent on the breeze."

"I'm happy I could provide you with help," she observed dryly.

He smiled, asking, "Did the good Captain finally come to his senses? Did you tell him what must happen so that you could finally return to your people?"

"No. I'm already with my people."

The wind-born gave a small shrug, his smile flattening out, "I was afraid of that." His voice developed a new edge, "But what can be expected of a half-breed raised in slavery by Samaya?"

"What?" Skylla's breath caught in her throat. The air suddenly filled with the scent of the ocean.

"You're tainted, Skylla, or didn't you know that truth?"

She just shook her head, the wind growing around her.

"That hair of yours tells the tale. You've got Samaya blood in you. The violet speaks of a true defilement of our species, the lasting effects of a forced union that leeched into your blood even as you formed in your mother's womb."

Bile rose in her throat.

"You're no Enlightened, just a foolish amalgam that has no true people or place to begin with. You may have gotten some of our gifts, so I tried to go against my wisdom on the subject to save you, but the taint was too strong."

"That's a lie," she whispered.

He turned his head, a finger rising to his ear, "What's that? Lies? No, I'm afraid all I have ever done it tell you the truth. But like every other time you didn't listen and now it's come to this.

"If you'd just listened to me, accepted my words, all this could have been avoided and your precious Captain and crew might have been spared. But no, you're ever the foolish girl."

She raised her nail gun, the weapon leveled at his chest.

The wind-born raised an eyebrow. "What are you going to do with that?" he asked.

Her hands shook, and tears welled in the corner of her eyes.

"I won't let you do anything to them!"

"The time for that has passed, now all you can do is save yourself. Stand aside, let me and my fellows destroy that cargo, and this can all just fade away.

"You may be a half-breed, and foolish, but you're young and I still care for you despite my better judgment. Just throw down the weapon and step out of the way and we can be together, at least for a little while."

Her jaw stiffened.

"Erik!" she proclaimed, half to herself

"What?"

"You knew the tale of Saint Erik, not because you venerated Shera but because he was your patron… you're a liar and a thief."

A charming smile washed across his face, a mocking bow following.

"A mystery solved, and it shows you have some promise," he said smugly.

She raised the weapon to her shoulder, steel in her voice, "Back away."

Raising both his hands Ethran casually flicked a finger. Wind ripped between them, the tendrils of air strong as a hundred men. Her gun flew from her hands, a discharged nail held in the air five feet from Ethran's left shoulder.

"You've no idea what I am," he whispered.

She took a step back, but the wind turned, a blast of it striking her like a sledge in the gut and sending her tumbling through the air.

Her lungs burned when she hit the ground, but she struggled to her knees, hair down over her face as her eyes searched beneath the Tyger. Kaleb stood against a wheel, his feet apart and arms crossed over his chest.

From the distance she couldn't see his eyes, but his hat tipped down in a nod and she sucked in a breath.

*I see you, I feel you… and I won't let you down again!*

Behind her the wind hissed, the air carrying with it the sound of a bone blade sliding from its sheath.

*Shera, thank you for this chance at redemption.*

Water dripped down her long strands of violet hair, her hand pushing off from the ground as she reached to her thigh and drew forth her twin knives.

Ethran was moving, legs parting the sea of grass as his dragonbone sword pointed like a lance at her.

Taking a blade in each hand, she turned them back until they rested against her forearms.

"And you've no idea what I am!" she whispered fiercely.

Ethran came forward, blade singing in the breeze, but she blocked the blow, struck with her left hand but he danced away, a blast of wind striking her eyes and forcing her back.

The wind-born's sword flashed out again, her knife blocking it an inch from her face. The parry left her unbalanced, and her off-hand went for naught as he pressed his advantage. His strikes came like an autogun's rounds, one after the other until he finally struck home, the blade's tip slicing a four inch line across her abdomen.

She winced, reversed her stance and threw her left knife, the blade striking a wind wall before dropping into to the grass.

"It's only a matter of time," he intoned fiercely.

A scream tore from her throat as she charged. Ethran backed away as he turned her attacks aside, before ending her advance with an outstretched palm that blasted her off her feet.

He was on her in an instant, the dragonblade falling toward her neck, but she rolled away, hair matted to her face and eyes streaming liquid.

Wind struck her again, blood spraying her cheek from a busted lip as Ethran danced back and saluted her with his blade, a mocking smile on his lips.

"You are under-skilled, ill-trained, and at a weapon's disadvantage. This will not end well unless you surrender yourself," he said.

She wiped the blood from her lip, the air playing around her, teasing her hair, brushing her naked skin where the bracers had recently rested.

Ethran smiled, a hand going out to one of his men, "Grego, see to the ship."

"No!" she screamed.

Ethran turned back as she brought her knife into defensive position once more.

"Foolishness," he whispered.

She charged, and he blocked her blade, but she caught him across the face with her left fist, his jaw cracking with the force of the blow.

He fell back a step, she lunged, but he recovered, lanced her across one thigh and disengaged. His eyes turned cobalt as he spit blood.

"That is your final mistake," he said.

Wind came forth in a gale force, her feet sliding across the ground as Ethran twitched his fingers, a cruel smile spreading across his bloody lips.

Her skirt tore away, hair blasted back and eyes forced closed as her lungs struggled to breath. She choked, twisted sideways, fell to a knee and crouched against the onslaught.

A ripple of congealed air shot through the wind, the edge traveling across the flesh at her shoulder and slicing her like a razor.

Skylla screamed with what air remained to her, another air-blade opening a wound in her calf. Slowly, with the sound of the tide coming in, water welled inside her as from a far off place, the power of it parting as a light forced itself through the tide. Its force came through her, jumping like a ground of electricity, and she threw her head back as a bolt of amber light shot from her chest.

The world shook, a thunderclap driving the point home as she split the earth and burned it asunder. Ethran dodged the blast, his cloak singed and the air falling away from her as she stood, the connection to the pure energy still pulsing though her bones.

"Wizard!" one of the Enlightened yelled.

They drew their weapons, and in reply shots were fired from the Tyger. The bullets struck an unseen air barrier as Ethran kept a hand raised.

Behind him, the Enlightened elements burst to life on the men's weapons – the blade and hammer shining with the display.

Skylla stood watching, eyes blazing as Ethran charged her again, this time in desperation. She lifted her hand, a blast of white-fire striking his blade and tearing it from his grasp.

He adjusted his rush, moving like an arrow to strike her across the face. She fell back. The air fought her, but she screamed and white energy broke the windy-bonds, flattening the grass around her and throwing Ethran onto his back with her outburst.

They both rolled, came to their feet, and crouched down as bullets struck Ethran's air shield. Behind them, the Enlightened charged, their conflict providing a misty backdrop as Skylla and Ethran opened their palms and brought forth the full force of their power against one another.

# CHAPTER TWENTY

## *KALEB*

*Y*ou wonder why I watch, why I wait. But what choice do I have?
*This is her high water mark, the definitive combat in her young life
that will shape everything about her going forward.*

*Yes, I know she could die, but we could all die, and as long as I see
this through, just as she is doing, we'll be better for it.*

*Now watch, whoever or whatever you are, and guide my hand to
make it true if that is in your power, but nonetheless keep faith that
what happens on this field today will be something of worth for years
to come...*

The Enlightened moved, two with swords blazing and one with a hammer smiting the ground. The Tyger shook before the elemental charge, as their final enemy, the man with a bow, drew back the string as air whipped around in his dark hair.

Above, a cannon fired, the shell caught like all the other projectiles at a point half the distance to the target.

Cursing, Kaleb drew his pistol and called up to Stoneham on the observation platform above.

"Archer!"

No sniper fire came, and the distant Enlightened released an arrow that carried a trail of mist behind it. The shaft sailed above Kaleb's head and there was an explosion of frigid air on the ship, a scream dying in a strangled clicking of ice.

Stepping from the shadow of the Tyger, Kaleb looked up. Ten feet of the port deck was covered in ice, the frozen form of Branson, rifle still held over the rail, stood like a crystalline statue.

Behind, an explosion rocked the field, and he adjusted his line of site to the observation deck. Jacob's arms and head hung over the rail, along with his rifle that was still attached by a strap.

*Assassin!*

Turning, he raised his weapon and marched forward. The two swordsmen were within thirty feet of the ship, and the hammer-wielder was another ten behind them. He leveled the pistol off, eyed down the barrel and let out a breath.

Beyond the charging foes, the archer reloaded, eyes going back to the Tyger as he raised the bow.

*Siegfried, guide my hand...*

The pistol's report was lost in the firestorm blast that shattered the ground around Skylla and Ethran. The archer lowered his bow, a hand moving to his chest before his knees buckled and then he fell forward into the grass.

Thumbing back the hammer, Kaleb adjusted his aim to the forefront of the charge, the heat of the charging men washing over him as the leader raised his great flaming brand over his head.

Another shot echoed, this one striking the lead swordsman in the face and spinning him sideways. Blood and heat spilled out into the air, Kaleb thumbing back the hammer once more.

"That's two, do you want to make it a third?" he asked.

The two remaining Enlightened pulled up short, weapons raised but eyes going to their fallen comrade who lay motionless in the grass.

"Your bowman is gone as well, so take stock. This isn't about you or me, it will be settled with the two on the field," he stated firmly.

The Enlightened, hard and tan one with eyes like shadowed ruby and the other polished onyx nodded and backed down. The smaller one, broad as he was tall, said something in a foreign tongue rich with flavor and rumbling like an earthquake.

The remaining fire-born turned, said something in the same language, and they moved back, each keeping an eye on the pistol still pointing at them.

Kaleb kept his weapon trained but let his eye wander to the combat. Skylla, half-naked and bleeding, was still showering the field with destructive bolts. Ethran was on a knee, his face blistered and his left arm a smoking ruin as he wove a series of windstorms and shimmering walls with his right hand.

She walked forward, almost fell, righted herself, and took three more steps as Ethran's arm slowly slipped to his side, his body tilting oddly until he tumbled over and lay still.

Kaleb kept the pistol on the other Enlightened, each taking steps away, their weapons now at their side or returned to their sheaths.

Skylla got only another step before she dropped to her knees, steam rising from her back, what remained of her clothes blackened to ash.

"Captain?" Tormay called from the port nacelle.

"Hold your fire!" Kaleb yelled.

He took a few steps forward, the ground near the combat nothing but smoking, baked earth. Skylla started crawling, one hand still holding a knife as she dragged herself to where Ethran lay.

When she got there she leaned down, the blade disappearing from Kaleb's sight as he quickened his pace, his boots kicking up smoke and ash as he ran.

Skylla put her head next to Ethran's, the Aspara reaching up with his right hand to touch her head as his lips moved. He whispered for a few moments and then fell back, his hand dropping to the cinders on the ground.

Kaleb came to a halt, his eyes dark as Skylla leaned up still staring down on the ruin of the man.

"He's dead," she whispered.

Kaleb reached down and grasped her shoulders, but she was dead weight. He knelt until he could place his arms beneath her and lift her up.

"Three-thousand years in this world, and I took his life in a matter of minutes."

She felt like a child in his arms, her eyes sunken and her bones and muscles wrapped so tightly by her ashen skin that she looked like a corpse.

Across the field the remaining Enlightened slipped into a defile and disappeared. He watched the horizon a moment, and then turned back to the ship, Skylla mumbling incoherently in his arms.

He was half way to the ship when Olaf met him, but he shrugged the Bosun off and continued to carry her until he got to the ship.

Doc Rose was waiting, bag in hand, and when Yogo took her at the top of the steps the two raced her limp body to the port deckhouse, Kaleb leaning heavily against the rail and staring at the frozen deck of his ship.

"Are you ok, Captain?" Greylin asked.

He nodded, eyes blinking before he looked up at the observation platform. Stoneham was standing, a hand holding his rifle and the other rubbing the back of his head.

"Go up there and see if Stoneham is ok," Kaleb ordered.

Greylin ran off, Olaf coming up the ladder to stand next to him.

"Another hard day," the Bosun commented.

Kaleb forced a smile, "You always did have a talent for understatement."

With that, he moved off the deck toward the bridge.

The Tyger rumbled down the bank into Storm Lake, the water parting around the pontoons and Kaleb leaning back into the Captain's chair. On the port deck, the ice steamed in the afternoon sun, the melt having spilled frigid water under the cargo tarp along the way.

Tormay, Greylin, and Olaf waited beside the ice with hammers, and Kaleb leaned into the ship's conical as they drifted out into the water.

"You can begin," he ordered.

The three men began hammering at the ice, the figure of Branson still frozen inside the icy tomb.

Kaleb stood, saying, "Mr. Gates, you have the bridge. Take her a hundred lengths from shore and then drop anchor."

"Yes sir," Morgan replied.

Kaleb slipped down to the starboard deckhouse, Mya was waiting for him but he waved her off and continued on to the deck and the infirmary beneath the nacelle. Light trickled in from the portholes, Doc Rose seated over a bed where Skylla lay. On another cot, Parish was propped up, his shoulder still covered in bandages.

"How is she?" Kaleb asked.

Rose sighed, "Really, I have no idea, other than she looks like death."

Coming forward, he stood over the two, Skylla's breathing shallow. She was pale, gaunt, and there was a tint of grey beneath her skin in places that looked like burns under the flesh.

"Parish, can you give us a moment?" Doc Rose asked.

Parish nodded, wincing as he got out of bed, but quickly slipped from the room.

Rose turned and took off his glasses, "I've never seen anything like this. And what she did out there, well…"

"It's Enlightened, I know, but that doesn't mean she's completely foreign to you does it?" Kaleb asked.

"No, but what happened to her is. If I didn't know better, I'd say she's been burned from the inside out, and I'm not sure her mind hasn't sustained damage as well. She keeps speaking, but her mumbles go from odd sentences, to gibberish, and then to nothing."

Kaleb continued to stare as Skylla's breathing became more and more labored.

"If you have something to say, I'd suggest doing it soon," Doc Rose whispered.

The doctor got to his feet, patted Kaleb on the shoulder and walked to the door. He paused a moment, saying, "If you need me, I'll be in the hall."

The door to the cabin closed and Kaleb took a seat.

"Three years! I really didn't think either of us would make it that long," he began.

Reaching out, he took her hand, her fingers like brittle bones wrapped in old leather.

"I shouldn't have taken off the bracers. If blame is to be had, I shouldn't even have taken the job in the first place. It was pride that swayed me, and now I've lost half my crew in the process. I understand they all knew the risks, but that doesn't mean I needed to put them in harm's way. Now it's all been for naught.

"Without you, we can't cross the final distance to the old Thalonian canals. I thought I had a secret weapon, your water magic all I needed to do the impossible..."

He lowered his head, ran his finger over her small palm and a bit of skin flaked off. He stared at it, picked it up and watched as it turned to dust between his fingers.

"Your water..." he whispered.

Standing, he slid his hands under her and pulled her from the bed. Her breathing hissed and stopped but he moved to the door and kicked it twice.

Rose opened it, "What's going on?"

"Out of my way!"

Kaleb rushed to the deck, Stoneham standing at the rail talking with Pascal and Tolbert.

"Drop the water stair!" he called.

They turned, looked at him but didn't move.

"THE WATER STAIR!"

The trio scrambled, Stoneham sliding down the deck until he pulled the clips from the rail door, Tolbert removing the tether lines form the stair that was mounted on the opposite side of the deck as he and Pascal pulled it free and ran it to the opening.

They forced it out, the steps striking the lake's surface with a splash. Kaleb did not break stride as he carried Skylla down into the water.

The lake was cold, turning his skin to gooseflesh as he dipped her into the gentle waves, her hair spilling out like a violet rose around her head.

"Breathe!" he whispered, half in command and half in prayer.

She lay still, and he dipped her below the surface, tiny bubbles dribbling from her lips.

"Come on, you're stronger than this!"

The water lapped at his chest. She looked serene in his arms, but did not stir.

"Kaleb, we can't save them all," Rose said breathlessly from the top of the stair.

He nodded, his hand going out to touch her face. His finger traced a line over her jaw and up her chin, until he touched the wound on her bottom lip.

At the contact, she jerked, her eyes flying open. Kaleb nearly dropped her, but she surfaced, drew in a great breath and then collapsed against his chest, shivering.

Her skin, once brittle was now wet and supple, and the flesh in her body had been restored. The skeleton he'd brought down the bridge now the strong young woman from an hour before.

She clung to him, her breath coming in great gasps until her breathing settled, her lips brushing his ear as she whispered, "The cores, Tiefon is going to use them to kill the Enlightened they've discovered on the Horned Isles..."

"What?" he asked.

Her head slipped down to his shoulder and her arms went limp. She said no more. Picking her up, he carried her from the water up the stair, the crew parting around him and Doc Rose shaking his head.

"It's a miracle," Rose said breathlessly.

Kaleb moved past him toward the infirmary, "No, it's magic, but to a Samaya a miracle sounds more palatable."

Stoneham sat across from Kaleb, the two men sharing a glass of Danric as the lantern burned low while a sound spinner played music on a table near the door.

"I had the archer in my sights and then everything went black," Stoneham said.

"Rose said you were lucky, a blow like that could have cracked your skull and left you addled for the rest of your days."

"Well, I always thought you and Skylla were the two hardest heads on the ship, but I guess mine's not far behind."

"That may be true, but I'm not convinced whoever did this was out to kill you," Kaleb said.

Stoneham took a drink, "I'd think if they wanted me dead, a knife would have done a better job."

"Perhaps, but whatever the case, someone on this ship was aware of what you had in that rifle and thought they should stop you before you used it."

"But the only ones who knew about the bullets were you and I," Stoneham said.

"Are you sure?" Kaleb asked.

"Meaning?"

"Meaning I know I didn't tell anyone, but I'm not the drinker you are," Kaleb replied.

Stoneham raised his glass, took a swig, "Agreed, Captain, but this is the first I've partaken of since we returned from the city."

"Unless you count Broken Branch," Kaleb said.

Stoneham smiled, scratched his chin, "Well, yes, other than that. But I promise you, Captain, I didn't tell a soul."

Kaleb nodded, "Well, it's a mystery then, and one I don't like having on my ship."

"A mystery with at least a few clues because Yogo, Olaf, Greylin, Tormay, and Gates were all on the port deck with rifles or at the cannon, and Branson is dead," Stoneham said.

"And Skylla and I were off the ship."

Stoneham rubbed the lip of the glass against his stubbled chin, "Which leaves Pascal, Ugarth, Tolbert, Doc Rose, Parish who was in the infirmary, and…"

"Mya," Kaleb finished.

The Captain looked at his desk, his journal and a pen lying atop the surface.

"Well, I wasn't going to include the Gola, but she was on board," Stoneham said.

Kaleb nodded, "Well, that's too many suspects for the moment, but keep your eyes open. One of them did this, and that means they're working for the Enlightened, or another force just as bad."

Stoneham finished his glass and got to his feet, "Will do, Captain."

Kaleb saluted him with a glass and the Quartermaster left, the door locking behind him. Rising from his chair, he went to his journal, untied the leather thong, and flipped through the pages. A quarter of the way through, a picture of a rune-inscribed bullet was drawn. The words 'Anti-Elemental Round' were written beneath.

*Ah Mya, I pray this isn't true…*

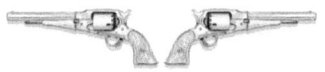

# CHAPTER TWENTY-ONE

## *SKYLLA*

*Sometimes it's hard to remember everything. Large chunks of the battle are lost to me, and I've been having headaches that stagger me in my tracks. Yet I live.*

*Kaleb saved me again. His knack at doing so is more frustrating than you can imagine.*

*The doctor says it was the water that brought me back, my spent soul somehow rejuvenated by it, but I don't think that's the case. It was him, I feel it in my bones, and the water was simply the healing presence I needed to facilitate the final step.*

*Still, something is gone from me. I spent it on that field, and I feel burned inside, tattered and torn like a fire raged within me and left me hollow. There's numbness in my fingers and I can't walk without help, but I breath, I live, and I smile when the mood strikes me...*

Two days had passed since she left the infirmary, Parish talking her ear off until she was moved out onto the deck next to the cargo tarps. The sun was warm, the breezes cool, and the spring played out in full bloom around the Tyger as it left the lake and started the journey east on land once more.

Kaleb had her placed next to the central box, the heat of the thing leeching into her as she closed her eyes and placed a hand against it.

Water flowed, but only a little, and each hour she found less and less power in her as the lake slipped further away.

Doc Rose did his best to keep her hydrated, but she flagged several times, and a heated argument raged between Rose and Kaleb until she was taken from the deck. Sleep took her, fitful dreams causing her to toss and turn among the sheets.

Kaleb visited her often, and she tried to get him to allow her back on the deck, but he just smiled and said "The doctor knows best."

On the fifth day, the ship splashed into the Mitrik River. Her pain eased and sleep finally came before she woke in the predawn, making her way unassisted to the deck. Mist played on the river's surface, shore birds chattering and the crimson stain of the Blood Moon still painting the horizon in the west.

"Should you be up?"

Skylla turned, Mya having come from the deckhouse to stand next to her at the rail.

"I'm feeling much better," she answered.

"That's good to hear."

They watched the water, the muddy brown surface stirring as insects bounced above it and an occasional fish splashed.

"Do you want to talk?" Mya finally asked.

"What do you and I have to talk about?"

"The city, Kaleb, your death and rebirth. There really is a lot you know."

Skylla let out a small laugh, "You just don't give up, do you?"

"I'm the Gola. This is my purpose."

Ahead, a bridge came into view, the thing a massive structure of cut, black stone and three huge arches set with central towers.

"We've made the Bridges of Alaron," Skylla said.

Mya turned and looked up at the oncoming structure, "Indeed we have, but that doesn't answer any question I'd like to hear."

"I'm not that girl, and I don't talk, especially to someone who knows my business and yet continues to place herself inside it," Skylla said.

"At least I've finally gotten a truth from you," Mya said.

Skylla pushed off from the rail, her finger rising up to point at Mya, "The Captain..."

Mya lifted an eyebrow, "The Captain, what?"

"He's mine, do you understand that?"

"Do you really believe that?" Mya asked.

Skylla looked at the weather-eye, the golden disk set in the front of the bridge between the pontoons staring down at her like an all-seeing Cyclops. She lowered her hand.

Mya continued, "I have a purpose, as much as you'd like to dissuade me from doing it, and until you get past that, we can't be friends. But remember, when you left him shattered, I picked up the pieces, even if only to return them to you."

Skylla paused, looked back at the river and sighed, "Friends? Are you serious? Do you really believe we could ever be?"

"Skylla, I'm not the enemy here. We're both slaves, so why do you hate me so?"

Skylla rubbed her arms where the bracers had been.

"Ladies," Kaleb's voice called from the deckhouse door.

They turned, Mya pulling her veil across her face and Skylla biting her lip.

"Captain," they said in unison.

"I didn't think either of you would be up so early. Skylla, did Doc Rose say you could leave your bed?"

She shook her head, "No, but I'm feeling much better and I wanted to go check on the cargo."

"It's fine, and I want you to stay the same, so what's say you head back and get some rest?"

She straightened up, green eyes flaring. There was a faint scent of ocean storms around her as she replied, "I'd like to resume my duties, Captain, as that's Alaron Bridge, which means Mitrik isn't far off. You'll need me at the drop."

"Ugarth is going with me to the drop. It shouldn't be a problem," he said.

"Ugarth? Captain, he might be a great negotiator, but I really don't think he's the one you need watching your back."

"And you're sure you can do that?" he asked.

"Yes,"

"I'm no doctor, but she looks well enough, Captain," Mya agreed.

Skylla looked at her, the woman's eyes downcast.

"Well, two ladies against one man, I'm afraid I can't argue with that," he said, holding up his arms in surrender. "Still, we won't make the drop till tomorrow night, so get some more sleep and I'll have a talk with Rose."

Skylla nodded, and Mya bowed before moving back toward her cabin. Kaleb stood a moment, his eyes finding places to rest other than on Skylla, before she took a step forward and kissed him gently against his cheek, stubble pricking her lips.

"Thank you," she whispered.

He said nothing and she quickly left the deck, her naked feet padding across the wood planks as she made her way to the infirmary.

The dock was lit with torches. A half-dozen men with rifles stood amid a collection of boxes as Kaleb spoke with a thin fellow in a domed hat.

She held her nail-gun at the ready, Ugarth beside her, his hat held at his waist and his left hand running through his well-oiled hair.

"I don't like the way this is going," Ugarth said.

"He'll wave you forward if he needs you," she replied.

"Still, this is a lot of firepower for a simple drop, even if our cargo is more than it might seem."

Skylla stood a moment before she turned to look at him, "What do you know about our cargo?"

His face was blank a second before he gave a cool smile, "I'm a member of the crew and we've been lugging this stuff across land for a month, when the ocean would have taken a quarter of the time. Doesn't that mean our cargo *has* to be some kind of interesting contraband?"

She frowned and went back to looking at the Captain. He and the other negotiator were growing more animated, the man continuing to point at an open crate.

"Have you thought more about my offer?" he asked.

"What offer?"

"You coming away with me once we settle up?"

"You're dreaming, and you should know that by now."

He nodded and the man in the dome hat shouting something at Kaleb before he turned and walked off. Several of the toughs stepped around him with weapons at the ready as they backed off as well.

Kaleb stood a while, watched the men disappear down the dock and then moved back to where they stood.

"Well, that didn't go as planned," he said.

"You should have called me up, Captain. It's my job to negotiate," Ugarth said.

"No, Mr. Ugarth, it's your job to find us work and smooth the rough edges of local administration, neither of which were involved in this particular meeting."

Ugarth shook his head as Skylla asked, "What was wrong with the shipment?"

Kaleb shrugged, "It looks like we were simply carrying old Samaya Proto-Cells, Fire Type, and not the Elemental Cores the traders claimed they'd uncovered in the Dragmarsh deadzone."

"But the cores were…" Ugarth broke off.

Both Skylla and Kaleb looked at the man, his cool smile returning before he continued, "...Elemental Cores... weren't they outlawed years ago, right, assuming you're talking about the ones used for powering large ships?"

Kaleb watched the young man, the two silent a moment before Kaleb said, "That's right, but it doesn't matter anyway since these were simply proto-cells. They're valuable, sure, but not the king's ransom we'd hoped."

"Captain... I was sure," Skylla began but he cut her off.

"You were wrong, and it wouldn't be the first time."

She nodded and he walked past her, Ugarth's face falling and Skylla sticking close as the three of them moved away down the dock.

"Mr. Ugarth, you stay here. I'll send Olaf and a couple other boys down to get the cargo. Once they make it to the dock, I want you to head into the district and see about selling them. It would be nice to get something for all this trouble."

Ugarth lagged back, "Yes, Captain."

Skylla waited till they made another turn, Ugarth lost in the tangle of crates behind, and then said, "Captain, you said we were shipping elemental cores."

"I know."

She shook her head, "But where? Why?"

"I dumped them in Storm Lake. We couldn't go on without you next to them, and once you told me their true purpose I couldn't see them delivered anyway. After I made the decision, I had our surplus of proto-cells loaded in the empty core container and hoped for the best."

She stopped and he went on several steps before he paused and turned back.

"Captain," she whispered.

"Yes?"

She ran forward and threw her arms around him, Kaleb falling back a step before he slipped his arms around her waist.

*Shera preserve, this feels like home.*

The smell of the deep ocean rose up around them, tinges of blue showing at her jaw, at the tips of her ears, and in her hands. Three years of unsaid words passed between them in that one embrace.

"Skylla..." he murmured into her hair.

She blinked away tears, closed her eyes, took a long breath, and then pulled away.

"Sorry, Captain, I just never thought…"

"What, that I'd give up a fortune for the Enlightened?" he asked, his eyes wrinkling at their corners.

She nodded.

"Well, as far as I'm concerned, the Enlightened have gotten an unfair reputation. The only one I know well is certainly one of the best people I've ever had the pleasure of calling a friend," he said.

To her right, two longshoremen stood watching, one of them whispering something to the other. She straightened up, drew her trench further around herself and nodded.

*Stay calm. Keep the water at bay…*

"You're a good man, Captain," she said.

He looked around, waved at the two men watching them, one of them waving back before the other slapped the man's arm down. The two exchanged heated words and Kaleb took her arm and led her away before the workers could recover.

"You keep talking like that, and my head won't fit through the door to the bridge. Besides, showing your water to the locals is a quick way to get us both killed," he said.

She drew close, took his arm and walked with him, both keeping silent as they leaned into one another all the way back to the Tyger.

# CHAPTER TWENTY-TWO

## *KALEB*

*It was a risky maneuver, and certainly a costly one considering everything we've done to get to this point, but I'm no murderer, nor will I be a part of genocide.*

*In making the switch, I had to paint myself the victim as well as the purchaser, and that meant arguing the point with dire fury instead of readily accepting a lessened payment. That gamble resulted in not getting paid at all, but it's a better result than having them believe I took the cores.*

*Yes, word will get back to the seller, but then again, Dragmarsh anarchists and Tiefon naval intelligence probably have no trust for each other anyway. In all likelihood they'll see conspiracies hatched by one another instead of one created by the broker involved in the exchange, especially if no outside seller produces the cores on the open market at a later date.*

*Still, word will get out that the Tyger showed up in Tiefon from the west, an unheard of proposition which is sure to bring more work, even if this trade turned out to be a failure. Such is the life of a free-booter captain, always on the edge of oblivion, but at least it makes things interesting...*

Kaleb sat in his stateroom, his journal in front of him and four torn pages beside it. He looked them over then turned to the candle beside him, touching their edges to the open flame.

They burned quickly, his hand turning them as they were consumed before finally dropping them into the tin tray next to him that held the ruined remains of a cigar.

A knock sounded on the door and he looked up, took a swig of Danric and then called, "Enter."

Skylla slipped inside the room. She wore her hair up, and was clothed in a dress of light blue silk, cinched at the bodice, wide at the skirt, with a neckline that plunged dangerously low. Gloves adorned her hands and pearls hung from her ears and her neck.

"Skylla?" he asked.

She took a long breath and smiled, saying, "I wanted to wear this before I came to you. I'd saved it for a few years, waiting for the day I could put it on without the bands."

He got to his feet, but she stayed by the door.

"No, you don't have to come closer," she said. "It's not like that. I just wanted to be someone I've dreamed about and longed to be my entire life, if even for a moment."

"Skylla," he whispered.

She shook her head, "It's stupid, and childish, but I don't really care. For years I've been aboard this ship and I've worn one thing and one thing only, my slave's attire. Now, my bands are gone, and I wanted to see what it was like to be what I always thought beauty was."

She ran a gloved hand down the tight waist.

"I guess what I've found is that it's damned uncomfortable."

She smiled and he laughed, taking another step forward but she held up a hand.

"Please, just let me finish."

He stopped, and she drew herself up with a breath, but even in lady's boots she only came to his throat.

"It's not for me, not that I could have it anyway. You were right, and even if the men on the docks don't report what they saw someone will at some point and then all this would end anyway.

"Still, you gave me a choice, which is more than anyone else in my life has ever done, and for that I can never thank you enough.

"After Ethran, I know I'm not fully of the Enlightened and that the deadzones are no blessing, nor is the freedom they provide. Freedom, I've come to realize, is in the heart, and the only place I feel that is on the Tyger, with the crew, and with you."

Reaching behind her she produced a frilly bag and offered it to him. He took it, opened the top and saw the oricalcum within.

"Skylla, you don't..." he trailed off.

She had reached behind her, fingers pulling at clips as the dress's frame gave way around her chest. She grabbed the sleeves, slid them off and let the fabric and boning pool around her feet. With a final flare, she pulled off the gloves, removed the earrings and necklace and then stood proud before him.

He stared, her body bronzed and naked, red lines on her skin were the dress had pressed her uncaringly, the only decoration left was her thigh sheath with its two long knives still holding on, and her high-heeled boots.

"I'm still yours, bought and paid for, and I want what's rightfully mine," she said as she held her hands forward.

He shook his head but she spoke again, this time with an edge in her voice, "Captain, if you don't do this I will die, as will you, and we've already lost enough. Claim your right!"

His hand slowly reached into the bag, fingers trailing against the cool metal until he drew out a bracer. She walked forward stepping over the dress and held out her arms.

He placed the first bracer against her left wrist, the metal bending like fabric as it looped around her arm until he pressed it together and the teeth closed without a visible seam.

The second bracer attached in the same fashion. She turned, took another step back until she was within a three inches of him, and then pulled her hair up another inch to fully expose her neck.

He took the choker out, dropped the bag and gently slipped the metal over her head before drawing it back into her neck. She leaned back further, pressed against him and his hands shook as he pulled the edges of the metal together, pausing a hair's breadth from closing it.

"Do it," she whispered.

He closed the clasp, three inches of metal stitching together until all sign of the breach disappeared.

She shuddered, and he put his arms around her. She held them, her fingers twining with his.

"I want you," he said.
"That will change everything," she whispered.
He kissed her below the ear, "I know…"

Author Scott Taylor has worked as a writer and editor of both fantasy and science fiction for the past decade and is currently the Senior Editor for Black Gate Books, a blogger for Black Gate Magazine's Website, and the founder of Art of the Genre Publishing. He lives in Ranchos Palos Verdes, California with his wife and son where he enjoys practicing a Peter Pan lifestyle.

David R. Deitrick is a former military man turned artist who has made a career out of defining role-playing games and comics since the early 1980s. He has worked on such classics as Star Trek, Battletech, Dr Who, Traveller and Space: 1889. He currently resides in Tennessee with his lovely wife Lori.